A Man Who Saw God

A NOVEL

A Man Who Saw God

A NOVEL

R.A. Singh

Raj Publications
New Delhi - 110002 (INDIA)

A Man Who Saw God: A Novel

First Published in 2007

ISBN: 81-86208-53-4

Published by : **Poonam Goel**

Raj Publications
108, 4855/24, Ansari Road
Daryaganj, New Delhi - 110 002

Tel. : 011 - 30120939

Laser Typesetting by : Tamalika Computers, Delhi

Printed at : Balaji Offset Printers, Delhi

PRINTED IN INDIA

Dedicated to

My dear brother in law
'Subhas', who was young,
smart and very promosing,
left us suddenly for the
'Heavenly' abode, bequeathing
two young children
(Pooja and Karan) to posterity.

PREFACE

My written work has generally been confined to professional subjects and occasionally to spirituality. My two books, which have already been published and are available to the readers; one is on 'India's National Security', highlights strength and weakness of our various national policies and measures to meet the challenges of new world order. The second book is 'A Quest for happiness', basically giving out a spiritual approach to solve maladies of human life. The work on these two books has been very satisfying and the response from the readers has been equally encouraging.

Since my above books are mostly based on facts and figures with my personal comments and ideas on these subjects, I wanted to change over to something creative and original. I read somewhere that there are certain essential qualities without which a writer can not become a successful novelist. In addition to basic talent, it has to be supplemented by his acquaintances with life. He can not portray life convincingly unless he is fully acquainted with it, rather he himself has lived it. Life provides to novelist raw material which he turns into a work of art with the help of his creative faculty. I was too delighted to find that I mostly meet these qualitative requirements for the kind of subject I had in mind for this book.

'A Man who saw God' covers issues on volatile socio-culture dilemmas and stark realities of life in the fast changing environment where value system is deteriorating. The book addresses most, if not all of the questions we have ever asked about life and love, purpose and function, good and evil, the path to God and road to hell. While writing this book, at places I was so emotionally involved that one was forced at time to carry out introspection of own life. I am sure the readers will also find this book very absorbing and interesting.

This book has been brought to shape with the help of many people. It is clear that all of us could produce a list of people who have touched our lives in ways so meaningful and so profoundly, as to defy categorization or description, people who have shared with us their wisdom and unfolded the truth of life. I shall be failing if I do not mention about my daughter in law (Yojna) who has been actively involved in production of my book, deserves a very special praise for her untiring and ever willing efforts. My wife (Rama) whose moral support and encouragement always make me going with my project,.also needs to be complimented.

R.A. Singh

I

Rajgarh a remote, desolate small village in district Sikar of Rajasthan lied quiet and defiladed among the sand dunes which were generally devoid of vegetation. It was connected by an unmettled road. The village mostly consisted of *kuchha* houses, thatched with cow dung and straw, which ran in continuous rows, swaying and billowing with streets. They were squat old houses, sagging at the shoulders, their faces haggard and cracked, like old women leaning against each other in disorderly queue at a government ration outlet. There was a small temple too in this village where people used to gather for their religious functions and other rituals. There was a general scarcity of public amenities except that the village had a school up to 8th class. The in-adequacy of portable water was conspicuous since women folk could be seen in groups with earthen pots going to community well to fetch water from a distance of approximately 2-3 kilometers.

The village was inhabited by number of casts ie Banias, (a trading community) Pandits, and others. The atmosphere in the village was calm and quiet and most of the local disputes were resolved by the Gram Panchayat. There was lot of harmony-religious, social and political among the communities inhabiting Rajgarh. People by and large were contented with the meagre income they had from their fields which mainly depended upon rains. The younger lot mostly moved out to cities for employment; even people went up to Tinsukhia in Assam for earning their livelihood. Though the village did not afford much opportunity for business ventures, however Lala Hari Ram of the same village belonging to trading community and traditionally committed to business, could manage running a grocery shop, income from which was just enough to meet his house hold expenses. He was short structured, a religious person who generally wore traditional dress, ie dhoti and kurta. he was a respectable person of the society. Though financially not very sound, but had acquired the reputation of being an impartial person with extra ordinary wisdom. People often sought his intervention in resolving family feuds in the village. His pious disposition impressed people and inspired confidence. Hari Ram was a man of integrity and could stand up to all odds. He was not afraid of defending his principles even if it was unpopular; all the same he was courteous and kind. He was highly emotional and sentimental person. He strongly felt bound to the society in which he lived and the future in which his children would live.

It was the month of April, weather was getting slightly warm particularly in this part of India. The village was full of activities due to conducive climate. Ox carts were moving around carrying farm products sack of grains while others were parked by the street sides. These carts moved two miles an hour, twenty miles a day, carried ton and a half of produce to market on their solid wood wheels. Queer-looking camel carts with large back wheels and cage like body, were part of the pageant of the tracks. Though they were no faster than the bullock carts, and carried half the load, but were still used extensively due to sandy terrain. In times to come it was thought that motors could displace camels and oxen but that time, only a few ramshackle buses plied on unmattled tracks, emitting clouds of oily smoke and carrying incredible loads.

There were lot of people coming to Rajgarh from adjoining places gathering at Lala Hari Ram's house. The day was slightly cool and pleasant, a few days ago there was heavy rain and some hail storm which partially affected the crops, but young wheat stood, the air was bracing and the green plains looked beautiful under the glitter of the spring Sun. The birds were flying around chirping, grey squirrel and rats ran skirmishing across the track.

Women in many coloured saris-glittering group of pink and daffodil and sky blue, with some black saris spangled with silver, seen moving around in the street near Hari Ram's house. Some of the children were dressed up in new clothes, some adorned with silver earrings were playing noughts and cross in the dust. There were some barefooted children playing with a very tattered rag doll which a considerate mother had patched up so that it should not shed its straws and others played with a stick made out by cutting a branch of 'kikar' tree and a ball made of rags and knit in strings. The men folk were dressed in best clothes, but the sunshine of month of April in Rajasthan pointed mockingly at their threadbare elbows and emphasized the shortness of their sleeves and all types of head gears. Some of the stray dogs were sitting and waiting for scrapes in front of Hari Ram's house. It was a big occasion for Hari Ram since he had been blessed with a son after three daughters, and it was the 'Nam karan' day of the newly born child who was just six days old.

There were lot of feasts and fire work around that house. There was a great happiness in Hari Ram's family with the birth of a male child since people in villages attach lot of importance and give preference to it. It was particularly so in Hari Ram's family since his son was born after three daughters. An elderly person, looked like a Pandit from the appearance, looked comparatively prosperous, riding on a horse entered the village Rajgarh. He was clean shaven, clad in homespun dhoti (a wide cloth hanging in folds from the waist and tucked in between the legs) and a khaki jacket. He wore a fine white turban, spectacles, country slippers and had a bamboo stick in his hand with a 'tilak' (white mark drawn on the forehead).

The Pandit was coming on a horse to perform the ceremony from the nearby village to Hari Ram's house that day.

Pandit ji asked a man who was going on a camel, "Can you tell me the house of Lala Hari Ram."

The villager smiled and said, "Pandit ji, you are on a good earning today, go straight and then turn right next to the temple, you will find lot of activities; that is the house."

Pandit ji—Why do you feel that I am here to make money? I am not a greedy person like other Pandits, I only believe in rendering free service to the community.

"Pandit ji has arrived," A young boy shouted in joy and went running inside the house of Hari Ram to inform them.

"Welcome Pandit ji," Said Hari Ram paying all respect to him and guided him to a small room nearby.

"No, I want to see the arrangements of the ceremony first," commanded the Pandit. "It is very important to check the layout and material required for the Havan," The Pandit further said.

"OK, come with me I shall show you everything including the arrangements that we have made for the feast for the guests also," Hari Ram said.

There was a bhajan mandli (singing songs) and on one side ladies sangeet was there. Children were clad in new clothes, running around singing and dancing. It was a special occasion for the complete village community for merry making and enjoyment.

"This is the room where we have kept the sweets made by the 'Halwai' and deshi ghee lamp after pooja was let burning inside," Informed Lala Hari Ram.

The Pandit ji was not too happy seeing pooja already done without his approval and said that pooja had to be done by a Pandit only otherwise the God will be unhappy and there will be shortfall of everything in this room.

"We have been doing it in this manner only in the past also," Informed Hari Ram.

"No, 'Nam karan' ceremony which includes 'havan' also will be treated as incomplete if you do not follow correct procedure," The Pandit said.

"OK, Pandit ji, please come and oblige us by your grace and perform the pooja of this room also," Said Hari Ram.

Pandit ji — Bring one kg deshi ghee and eleven rupees for the pooja. By making offerings to God we multiply instead of deviding out wealth.

"Yes, Pandit ji, it is here for you to proceed," Hari Ram spoke in all humility.

The Pandit ji carried out his normal Nam karan ceremony and the newly born was named as 'Madan' based on the kundali (horoscope) of the child. During the 'Havan' (fire lit in an iron container) the Pandit chanted religious songs and holy verses from Hindu scriptures which were often repeated by the audience. He discoursed on philosophy of life. The essence of 'Pandit hood' seemed to lie in one's ability to utter mystifying statements. He tried to drag those innocent people deeper and deeper into bog of unclear thoughts, more so to acquire a reputation of a knowledgeable Pandit in the society and area around. The ceremony went on well and everyone in the village including the guests enjoyed every bit of it. The pooja began and finished using only 50 gms of deshi ghee, rest the Pandit ji took possession of, including eleven rupees. All the guests were served lunch as part of the feast. It was about 2 PM when the function got over. The sun was shining outside in all its glory in the month of April in Rajasthan. The guests were oppressed by the heat. It was awefully hot in the afternoon. The streets were dreary and deserted and only the visitors around Hari Ram's house could be seen. Some birds were twittering on a tree and an odd squirrel could be seen crossing the track. All visitors were perspiring profusely. The guests who had come from other villages were moving on their horses and camels, their heads covered with turbans to beat the heat. The local guests were rushing towards their houses to seek asylum from scorching heat. The sun was without beauty.

The summer season is a season of horror in India and it makes people lazy and sluggish. They lose the power of resistance and are easily enslaved.

II

Lala Hari Ram had four children, one son and three daughters. Madan was the youngest child. Hari Ram's small shop of kiryana (grocery) in his village was only the source of income to sustain his big family. Shanti was the name of Hari Ram's wife who was very pious and religious lady. She would get up early in the morning at 4 AM daily, finish her normal routine, do up the house and by the time children woke up, she would even finish her prayers. It was a very happy family with lot of love and affection among them. They were very courteous, any visitor was always greeted with smile. The family was a model in the village because of their behaviour and conduct and everyone respected Lala Hari Ram despite his economic condition being not very sound.

Lakshmi was the eldest of Hari Ram's children. She was studying in class VIII and her other two sisters were also in the same government middle school of the village in various classes. Lakshmi used to help her mother in daily house hold routine before going to school. Shanti was very proud of her pretty, well behaved elder daughter Lakshmi. The three sisters used to go together to the village school.

Though sending girls to school was not very common in that village, but Hari Ram despite the resistance from the villagers did not stop his daughters going to school along with the boys.

Madan, since childhood was a very active child who was being taken care of by the entire family, particularly the female members. Lakshmi the eldest daughter of Hari Ram was very much attached to this child and as Madan grew she started taking him out of the house for play and walk. Lakshmi was very fond of Madan and she showered all her love and affection on him.

As Madan was growing his habits were slightly different from other children. He would not accept any eatables from outside and instead offer his share of eats etc. to his friends or other children. When he was about three years of age, his curiosity in godly matters grew and he would ask difficult question from his parents particularly relating to 'Bible' of which none in the village had any clue. Madan used to get thrilled whenever he heard the bells ringing in the temple of the village. One day he disappeared from the house in the night and everyone got worried and started looking for him. Hari Ram was just passing by the temple looking for Madan that he noticed a child sleeping on the stairs of the temple. He woke up the child and found that was his son Madan. "What are you doing here," Asked Hari Ram. "I enjoy working and staying here near God." Replied Madan. Hari Ram asked the boy to come, home, telling him that the God is everywhere including our house.

Even later Madan often repeated going to the temple and sleeping on the stairs. He used to talk of Bible and Christ at the age of five. This put the family totally off, doubting influence of some ill spirit on the boy. They took Madan to number of 'tantriks' who they thought could resolve the mystery, but all in vain. Hari Ram was often annoyed by Madan's abstinacy to run to the temple in that manner.

Now that Madan was five years of age, he was admitted to the village school. There were a number of boys of his age with whom he fast befriended. His sisters were also studying in the same school and Madan used to accompany them to the school. One day all of them were going to school and suddenly hearing the bell of the temple Madan ran towards the temple leaving everyone. His second sister Sushma ran behind him to the temple; frightened.

"Why have you come here," Asked Sushma, sweating. "I do not know what happens to me when the bell of temple rings, I want to run and stay in the temple," Replied Madan. Sushma said, "we are getting late, let us go to the school." Thereafter they went to the school.

The school was a square, sad looking brick building. Madan was led into a classroom which was full of boys. It was a long room where three lines of floor mats were organized for the students to sit. Bits of paper lay on the floor. The walls was covered with ink as if rain of ink had come through the roof and there was an unpleasant smell in the air.

Madan joined the youngest and most elementary set just learning the alphabet and numbers. The teacher made them read aloud from their books and copy down the letters on their slates. The teacher then looked through each and gave them correction and flicks from the cane for those who repeated their follies. The teacher was comparatively an old person nearing his retirement, who was very strict and abusive and habitually addressed his pupils as dirty dogs and traced their genealogies on either side with thoroughness.

The boys also made lot of noise and as soon as the teachers back was turned and he had gone to his house in the school itself, they rolled over each other, fought, scratched, bleated and yelled. Once even they invaded his privacy by entering the kitchen and found him cooking. They all giggled and the old teacher was furious. Henceforth they were all forbidden to enter his house.

The boys brought to their teacher presents of eatables frequently and even he himself asked children to bring articles from their homes whenever he needed. The parents were also glad to oblige him for he kept them in his charge for nearly the whole day and thus relieved them of the trouble at home.

Madan was intelligent. He did well at the school and was promoted to the higher class. The old teacher blessed his students and the children were pleasantly surprised to see that he could be so kind also.

Madan liked his father's habit waking him up with the crowing of the cock and then teaching him arithmetic before he went to school with his sisters. Hari Ram would take Madan to town sometimes when he went there to make purchases for his shop. He would make Madan sit on a wooden platform with in sight of a shopkeeper known to him and would go about to do his shopping. Madan would look fescinated at the changing scene, men, women, children, carts on the move around him, till he would feel drowsy and go to sleep.

Madan was showing keen interest in his father's business, as he was growing. At mid day during school break his father would call Madan when Hari Ram went for lunch. Hari Ram would tell Madan, 'take my seat, be sure to receive the money for whatever you give. Do not eat off all that eatables, it is kept for sale, call me when in doubt. Whenever customers came and Madan was in doubt about the rate, he would call his father aloud asking for the rate which Hari Ram would reply, which sometimes involved complicated concessions, which Madan could apply intelligently. The shop remained open till late in night. Late customers and Hari Ram's friends would sit with him for hours discussing sundry topics as the price of grains, rainfall, prospects of good harvest or they would talk of their litigations and talk would go on endlessly. Hari Ram at times would forget about his food till his wife sent for him for dinner. Madan used to be told stories by his mother till he went to sleep. He preferred listening to religious stories and often bring in some point concerning either '*Bible*' or '*Lord Jesus*' abruptly. Though he could not sustain this conversation since he would very vaguely recall and then fail.

Lakshmi, the eldest daughter of Hari Ram had finished her education and Hari Ram was looking for a suitable match for her. Hari Ram used to be under tension for two reasons, one to find a match for Lakshmi and other one being Madan's erratic behaviour.

"Why are you morose father," Asked Madan.

"No, I am not morose I am just thinking about your eldest sister Lakshmi. The boy that was told by the neighbours are asking lot of dowry which we can not afford," Replied Hari Ram.

"Go and pray to God, He will help you to find a match soon. He never lets down his 'bhakts'," Said Madan, very confidently.

Hari Ram could find a suitable boy for Lakshmi, who was though from a close by village but was working in Assam with other 'Marwaries'. The marriage was fixed to be solemnized in Rajgarh only. Hari Ram always worked within the framework of traditional Hindu society and he endorsed its code of conduct.

"Barat (marriage party) has come and the groom is very handsome," Announced one of the ladies of the village in excitement.

"OK, let us go and organize reception of the Barat. Madan, you also come with us to the gate, hold that horse with you which will be needed for the groom," 'Said Hari Ram.' Right father, I shall do it, you take care of the other things, Said Madan.

As per the customs in Rajasthan, once the Barat reaches the outskirts of the village, it waits there only till some people from the village receive and welcome them. Either a Pandit or a barber from the barat is sent with a green branch of a tree (Hari Tehni) to bride's house to inform about the arrival of the barat. Once this barat was received, it was moved to village school where arrangements for their night stay were made. The barat was also served with hot tea, soft drinks and some snacks and sweets soon on reaching the school complex. After the refreshment the bridegroom along with the barat was to move to bride's house for performance of 'Darwaza' gate ceremony. By then all the member of the marriage party had changed to their best robes and for the groom, the horse duly decorated was held by Madan in the school complex itself. It was evening and the bell started ringing in the temple for normal evening prayers. Hearing the bell, Madan got excited and not caring for the responsibility of holding the horse, he let it loose and ran towards the temple. This surprised everyone including the marriage party who by then had gathered to move to the gate of Hari Ram's house. Nobody followed Madan this time since it had become a kind of routine habit of Madan for the family and the marriage party in anycase were not aware of this kind of reaction from Madan when the temple bell rang. Normal marriage ceremony went on. Madan returned himself after nearly two hours when most of the functions had got over. Seeing Madan, Hari Ram lost his temper and started beating Madan, which hurt Lakshmi (the bride) the most, who loved and cared too much for Madan.

"Do not beat the young child who is so innocent," Said Lakshmi, to her father.

"He ran away even at such an auspicious occasion when his eldest sister who loved him so much was getting married. Does he deserve any sympathy? Said Hari Ram in anger.

"I can not help this, I do not know what happens to me when the bell of the temple rings," Replied the weaping child.

"There appears to be some ghost troubling this young child, who makes him behave like this," Told one of the old looking man from the marriage party.

"There was a similar case in our family when a young girl used to cry at night without any reason and she was treated by a Sadhu who lived in an ashram in Tinsukhiya," The old man further said.

"If this young boy is taken there, I am sure he will become alright," Added the old man.

"Yes we will take him there," Said the groom, Mr Navrang before Lakshmi could say anything.

"Father please send Madan with us, this will keep me also a good company and we will get him well," Added Lakshmi.

Hari Ram had got emotional by then seeing his only son crying because he beat him up for reasons which were beyond Madan's control. He after pondering a lot and deep on his future, hesitatingly agreed to the proposal from his son in law and daughter for the good of his only son.

Madan was delighted at the prospect of seeing the country side and the train in particular about which he had only read or heard from his mother; yet he was slightly unhappy also seeing his mother weeping and father also in tears.

"Father if you feel I should not go then tell me accordingly, I shall stay here with you and try not to run to the temple. But do not shed tears, I can not leave you like this," Said Madan.

"No son, these tears are because of your sister Lakshmi's departure from this house to another house, that thought is troubling me." Hari Ram replied.

The marriage party left early in the morning to catch train from Delhi for Assam. It was quite enjoyable for Madan since it was his first outing from a small village of Rajgarh.

New Delhi Railway Station where large number of trains were going and coming amused Madan. He had seen buses and cars which used to often come to his village, but so many compartment each of a size of a bus connected together, being pulled by one engine, on two separated tracks was a big experience for Madan. To satisfy his curiosity he was asking some silly questions which were due to his ignorance, from his brother in law, Mr Navrang. Madan preferred to take on a seat close to the window when they boarded Tinsukhia Mail at New Delhi railway station. His sister Lakshmi, though still feeling home sick was particularly caring for Madan. Navrang was no less caring, he would give lot of toffees and sweets to Madan to eat. This all probably made Madan forget his village and parents left behind at Rajgarh, for the time being. Train started. Everyone of the marriage party settled on their respective berths in the train.

"How long will it take us to reach Ṭinsukhia Jija ji," Asked Madan.

"It will take almost three days and three nights including one change to another train on meter gauge at Gauhati, which will take us to Tinsukhia," Navrang told Madan.

"Where will we eat, take bath and go for nature's call for these many days?" Asked Madan very innocently.

"Do not worry, it is all inside the train and we are carrying lot of food to eat and also we would buy some from the railway stations enroute, where ever the train stops," Replied Mr Navrang.

Night fell. Madan went to sleep. He had got tired travelling since morning from his village and then kept awake looking outside the window in the running train the whole day. He had sound sleep and got up when woken up by Lakshmi the next morning. The environment and activities in this reserved III Tier compartment were very delightful for young Madan who was just six years of age. He had known everyone of the marriage party by then and all showed special love and affection to this child. There were a few boys of similar age group in marriage party, who also became friendly to Madan. The whole day, these boys kept exchanging notes among themselves and Madan was apparently feeling at quite an ease. Second night fell, this time Madan knew the complete drill and his berth to sleep. Having had his dinner which was got from Railway kitchen car, he went to sleep.

It was past midnight, the train had entered Assam, Madan woke up all of a sudden and sat up on his berth, breathing fast. This disturbed the sleep of Lakshmi who was sleeping on the adjoining berth.

"What has happened Madan, why are you so frightened," Asked Lakshmi.

"It appears, I have been to this area earlier and have travelled on this route," Said Madan who was still breathing fast and feeling slightly uncomfortable.

"No, Madan, it seems you have seen some bad dream and you are still a child, how could you have been here earlier in this area. Go to sleep," Said Lakshmi, her tone hushed with humility and fear but her manner was earnest.

Madan again went to sleep. It was raining very heavily through-out the night along the entire route, with lots of lightening and thunder. It was about 5 AM in the morning and the train was entering Rangiya railway station. Madan again suddenly got up and started running towards the gate of the train to get down.

Lakshmi who saw Madan moving towards the door, woke her husband also and started following Madan.

The train stopped at Rangiya Railway Station, there was incessant rain, with thunder and lightening. There was also no light on the railway station except with the gate keeper who could be seen with a lantern in his hand sitting on a stool in one corner.

Madan got down and started running out of the railway station without caring for the rain or the darkness.

"Madan where are you going? Stop, it is dangerous area with lot of wild animals," cried Lakshmi who was following Madan.

"Do not come with me, I know this area well; go back," Replied Madan recklessly while running.

Madan headed straight for an old church which was about 300 yards from the railway station, in an isolated area surrounded by lot of high trees and foliage. He climbed the stairs of the old church and started shouting Papa, Papa, knocking the doors of the church. Having had no response from inside the church, Madan then went to the out house of the church where the priest lived. He knocked the door of that quarter and one old man came out.

"Father, Good morning, I am David. Don't you recognize me?" Madan asked the Priest who had just come out of the quarter.

"Who David? I do not remember anyone by this name," Muttered Father in amazement, gazing at him with intense curiosity.

In the meantime Lakshmi and her husband had also reached the scene and they requested the Priest for excuse since Madan had disturbed him at the odd hour.

"He is mentally slightly upset Father, please forgive him. He was talking irrationally in the train at night also, we are taking him for the treatment to Tinsukhia", Told Lakshmi, very humbly.

"No, let the boy speak whatever he wants. Don't stop him," Priest said.

"Father, I am David son of Mr Albert who is also a priest here. My mother is Maria, they live in this quarter only. You used to visit us from Missamari church very often," Told Madan reflecting on episode in retrospect.

"Yes son, proceed, tell us something more about you," Asked the priest.

"I was studying in 8th class in St Joseph school here when I met with an accident and died about seven years ago, near Police Post which is close to the school," Madan told the priest. There was an old sweepress who had been working in the church for over 50 years, was also staying in the adjoining room of the out house. She was also listening to the whole conversation. She came out with the help of a stick barely managing her way out in the rain and darkness. She was totally puzzled but moved close to Madan.

"Amma, Geeta, I am David, do you remember me? Where are my parents," Asked Madan crying and hugging Geeta the old lady.

The old lady sighed deeply, trying to control her emotions.

"Leave her Madan, do not cry, they all are strangers, we do not know them, come, let us go otherwise we will miss the train also," Said Lakshmi pulling aside, pacifying Madan.

"No, I am not Madan, I am David, there are no strangers here, this is my amma, Geeta who used to lookafter me and escort me to the school. He is father Rodrigues, who is our family friend and often comes to my father from Missamari," Retorted Madan, pulling away his hand from Lakshmi.

"Father do you remember, one day you came by night train and the weather that day was like this only. I was sent by my father to bring you home. Since it was raining we hired a rikshaw. As we were nearing our house one of the wheels of the rikshaw came out and you fell on the road and I fell on you. Your right elbow got fractured," Told Madan.

"Yes my child I remember you well," said the priest emotionally and hugging Madan. "Come inside my son, we will talk there," Further said the priest.

They all went inside the house with the father. The train in the meantime had left. Two more members of Navrang's family had also got down and joined the newly weds at the church. Lakshmi was crying badly seeing the state of her only brother whom she had so affectionately cared for. The fear of losing her brother was terribly haunting her. The worry writ large on her face.

"Do not cry my child, the boy remembers his last birth which he now recounts. It is a case of reincarnation and he will be alright," Told the priest to Lakshmi.

"He used to run to temple on hearing the bell ringing there, in the village also, and we are taking him for the treatment to Tinsukhia since we doubt some ill spirit haunting him," Informed Lakshmi.

"No my child, you are mistaken, he is perfectly alright, he needs no treatment. There are number of cases of this kind where people remember their last birth, but forget it soon as the time goes by," Said the priest.

They all moved inside the house. Madan recognized everything, indicated his room, his father's room and his mother's, and younger sister Alex's room. He went to his room and started inspecting everything including doors, windows, fans and the other permanent fixtures.

"Father how did you manage to open the store room of the church since the keys on that day were with me and I forgot to give it to my father," Told Madan.

Madan remembered keeping the keys in an open space above the almirah, and he took these out, which were fully rusted by then and handed to the Priest.

"Yes my son, these are the keys of the store room. After you left, your father got duplicate keys made and opened the store. It remained closed for a few months since there was a mourning on your death," Said the priest.

"Where are my parents and sister Alex, you have not told anything about them as yet," Querried Madan emphatically.

"It is again a tragic story my son. After your death, your parents were totally broken. Maria, your mother did not eat for days together. She fell very sick. Your father Albert could not alone manage the house and the church. Though father Rodrigues did help them very often visiting them from Missamari," Told Amma Geeta, putting her hand on Madan's head.

"But where are they now," Hurriedly asked Madan.

"Your mother could not bear the shock of your sudden death, she got into acute depression. She was taken even up to Gauhati for treatment but it did not work. Your father had also got helpless; Alex continued her schooling, mostly staying with me," Explained Geeta.

"What happened to them, tell me fast amma, I am losing my heart," Said Madan.

"Someone suggested a change of place as one of the remedies for your mother's ailment and your father had no choice but to shift out of here," Told Geeta.

"Where have they gone? Where is Alex? please tell me," Begged Madan, bursting into louder sobs.

"They went to Calcutta from here. There was a regular communication from your father for two-three years. But I was told thereafter they left Calcutta also and probably shifted to Nepal," Told the priest.

"Do you have their address or know their whereabouts," Asked Madan.

"No son, after leaving Calcutta, your father did not keep any contact. Though your mother had improved slightly and Alex was continuing her studies well, that was the last news we had of them," Said the priest.

Hearing all this Madan started crying, remembering his parents and visualizing what conditions they would be in. Lakshmi and her husband held him in their laps, soothing him. Amma Geeta, was also assuring Madan not to worry for them.

"Will he be alright now father," Asked Lakshmi, who looked dishevelled and her eyes were red with recent tears.

"Yes, of course he will soon be alright. He is the boy who spent most of his time in the service of God, helping his father in his last birth, before he departed prematurely, but how could ill spirit haunt such a noble soul," Told the priest, asking Madan to go with them.

"No I shall not go," Insisted Madan.

"Son, this is your second birth. You are now Madan and not David. Look how loving your sister is. You have your parents at home who would also be missing you badly. What you remember is the story of your past life," Advised the Priest.

Geeta once again hugged Madan and kissed him. Father Rodrigues blessed the child for a long life and prosperity. They then all left the church for the railway station to catch the next train for Tinsukhia. Madan was sad and generally quiet. At this stage Madan who was afresh with his last birth, was feeling slightly lonely and dejected.

Lakshmi, her husband and others caught another train from Rangiya for Tinsukhia. The journey was about one more day and one night with a change of train at Gauhati. Madan remained generally composed through out the journey but often raised queries about his past parents and became sad. Lakshmi and her husband Navrang however were able to manage him and reached Tinsukhia.

There was a crowd of relatives and family member at the railway station of Tinsukhia to receive the newly weds. Madan also got excited and happy seeing such a large gathering including some of the boys whom he had befriended during the train journey. Everyone was particularly caring for Madan since they all had known of his story of reincarnation.

"Come my son, this is also your house, feel totally relaxed," Told mother of Navrang to Madan.

"Yes, Mausi ji (mom), I am alright now. I am going to play with Raju, (a boy who had become his friend), you don't worry," Said Madan.

There were lot of celebrations in the house including certain rituals to welcome the new bride. Day passed well. Madan also was enjoying and playing with his friends. Next day was the reception party where lot of outsiders including guests were invited. There was display of band, a place for dance and good seating arrangements was made. Everyone was enjoying the celebrations, so was Madan. Lakshmi though was be-seated alongside her husband Navrang, but more than enjoying the festivities of the function, she was keeping an eye on Madan who was also busy dancing with the children.

"See Navrang, Madan seems to be forgetting his past life, how nice to see this change in him" Said Lakshmi to her husband.

"Yes, with God's grace he should be alright soon, but we must take him to that saint in the ashram tomorrow to know if anything else is still needed to be done to help Madan get absolutely well soon," Replied Navrang.

Next day as planned, Madan was taken to the Saint who was not a 'tantrik' but an old, learned and knowledgeable person, a total renunciate, fully devoted to God, staying in an isolated ashram in jungle. There was always a gathering of people in the ashram, a few would prostrate since the saint was rendering free and selfless service to the community. As Madan entered the ashram, the saint smiled at him and asked him to come and sit next to the saint.

Keeping his hand on the head of Madan the saint said, "You are alright now, forget your past, concentrate on your present, this is the life for you for which the God has sent you again on this earth. He is testing you this time."

"Baba, will he be alright," Asked Lakshmi, submissively.

"Yes, he is already alright, you do not have to take him anywhere, nor should you talk to him on this subject. Such cases of reincarnation do occur and people remember their past life. But soon after meeting the last family, one gradually forgets the past, this is the law of the Nature," Said the Saint. They after taking the blessings of the Saint, returned to their house.

Madan got busy in playing with his friends as a routine and he started liking Tinsukhia which is reasonably a big city. One can find a lot of 'marwaries' (trading community from Rajasthan) settled here. They control most of the business, not only in Tinsukhia, but in other big cities of Assam, Meghalaya and practically in the entire North-East region. They are even found doing small business in the remotest corner of this part of the country. There are a very orthodox community and what has helped them maintain their identity is that they severely abhor inter caste marriages and immediately outcast a person who violates these norms of their 'marwari' society.

Tinsukhia the last railway station, was connected by a meter gauge line from Gauhati. The city had all the public amenities including good schools, colleges, hospitals and cinema halls. Madan who saw electricity in her sister's house and water coming out of the taps for the first time in his life was too amused and infact played with flushing out water in the toilets even without use. Lakshmi would particularly ensure that Madan was not allowed to feel solitary and he was normally taken out to market and sometimes for seeing a motion picture in the cinema hall. Rakesh was one of the boys who was spending his holidays in Tinsukhia with his relations, had become good friend of Madan. Rakesh's family lived in Tezu in Lohitpur division, of Assam, across river Brahmaputra, a far flung place. His father who after attending Navrang's marriage had returned to Tezu to look after his canteen which he ran on contract for the army troops in that area. Now the schools were re opening and Rakesh was waiting for his father to pick him up.

"Madan, my father has come to take me. We shall go tomorrow early morning so to avail first ferry (a big motor boat) across Brahmaputra at 8 AM otherwise the next turn would be after 10 AM and we will get late with that, reaching Tezu by that evening." Told Rakesh.

Madan was little disappointed to learn about the departure of his friend Rakesh; though it was not sudden since he expected Rakesh to depart for his schooling at Tezu, for which both of them used to pray for as much delay as possible.

"What is this ferry over river Brahmaputra you are talking about," Asked Madan, innocently from Rakesh.

"There is no bridge over river Brahmaputra. It is approximately two miles in width, particularly now, during rainy season. There are big boats which are capable of carrying up to 20 people and even one or two vehicles depending up-on its size, across the river. These are called ferries," Told Rakesh.

"These ferries have timings like railways for departure, unless of course these are delayed due to floods or rise in river water," Further said Rakesh.

"Will you all take me up to the ferry site at river Brahmaputra," Asked Madan from Rakesh.

"Yes, there is no problem. My Uncle is taking his jeep to drop us upto the ferry. But you will have to ask your sister or brother in law for the permission," Told Rakesh.

Madan was thrilled and went running to his sister Lakshmi to seek her permission. Lakshmi readily agreed and spoke to Navrang, her husband to accompany Madan and show him around the country side. Navrang who was already thinking of taking Madan to tea gardens someday, found this an opportune movement. As per schedule they all left next morning at 6 AM to reach the ferry site well in time, which had just an hour running time in a jeep.

Having reached the ferry site, they all got down including Madan. Madan was getting curious to know about the mystery and vastness of river Brahmaputra which lied ahead as a formable adversary to be negotiated. There was one army jeep also in the waiting to be ferried across with some men in disruptive army uniform standing near it. Father of Rakesh bought tickets from the counter for him and Rakesh, which cost four annas each.

"Is there still land other side of this water," Asked Madan from Navrang, who had lot many questions to ask about this unique phenomenon of the nature.

"Yes, of course there is land across. The ferry would take about forty five minutes to reach the other side. Then these people, including Rakesh and his father would get into buses and jeeps waiting other side of the River to travel further to their destinations by road," Explained Navrang.

There was an army jawan in the hearing distance of Navrang and Madan's conversation. He having been prompted by the innocence of the young lad, got close to Madan and wanted to brief the boy voluntarily about what laid ahead up to the border with China. Seventy percent of man in the Indian Army come from Northern India and when they find someone in such a remote area belonging to their part of the country or area around, they show extra courtesies and are very hospitable. This spontaneous reaction on part of that army jawan to brief Madan was part of that natural habit.

"Yes uncle, please tell me quickly before it is time for you to leave," Requested Madan to the army man.

"Son, India is a very vast country with interesting terrain configurations. After we cross river Brahmaputra, we will unload our jeep and travel by road up to another water channel called 'Degaru Nala'. It will be around lunch time that we would reach there. If the water level is up to the acceptable limit then our jeep would be pulled across by an elephant which is employed by the government for this job. Having got across then we will reach Tezu (Lohitour) by the evening; of course there are a few more small water channels enroute, where help of small ferries are taken to get across, if the water level is above fordability of the jeep. That is how we and your friend Rakesh (who by then had joined Madan) would reach Tezu," Said the army soldier.

"Is Tezu located on the border with China," Asked Madan.

"No son. The border is about over one hundred kilometers away from Tezu," Replied the soldier.

"But you said you will tell me as to how you reach the border," Asked Madan.

"From Tezu we travel in a vehicle up to 40 kms to a place known as Chakvanti, the road-head. From here actual mountainous terrain starts. From there we walk for two days on foot to reach a small place in the valley known as 'Walong'. There is a small air field also there where defence aircrafts land. It takes just one more day on foot to reach Kibitoo, last village on the Indian side of the International border. In fact in this area, borders of India, China and Burma meet;" Told the soldier.

It was now time to board the ferry. Everyone including Rakesh his father and the army soldiers along with their jeep, got on the ferry. As a drill everyone was asked to open their shoes laces; to cater for the eventuality of any mishap while wading through the river. The shoes are a big hindrance in swimming.

Madan got emotional while bidding good bye to Rakesh and tears rolled down his cheeks. Navrang could well understand the value of the sentimentality between two good friends, parting company. He pacified Madan and after sometime the boat reached an un identifiable distance. They all returned to Tinsukhia in the same jeep.

Few months past, there was a call from Madan's parents to get him back home and Lakshmi was also asked to come to meet her parents for a few days, after her marriage. As customary Lakshmi, her husband and Madan came to Rajgarh. There was no reaction of any kind from Madan in the train particularly when they passed through Rangiya; though it was night time and he mostly was remembering and talking about meeting his parents and other two sisters. The story about Tinsukhia was often matter of his conversation enroute.

III

Madan was very happy having returned to his village. His father Hari Ram was still worried about the health of his only son Madan. But Lakshmi had narrated the entire episode to her father and that Madan was perfectly alright. However she cautioned her father to be little careful about the young boy and that no one should try and ask him questions on his past life.

Life in the village continued as usual. Madan also rejoined his school. He had generally forgotten his past life, nor were there any reactions by him on hearing the bell of the temple ringing as used to happen earlier. Hari Ram's kiryana shop was just doing average to meet the expenses to run his family.

Madan also used to help his father Hari Ram in running the small shop. Infact he was more keen sitting in the shop doing business, then to play and waste time with his friends. As he grew he used to give suggestion to his father how to increase the income from this shop by still increasing the provisioning. But it could not be done since his father had other responsibilities of marrying two grown up daughters who had already finished their 8th class education in the village school, a long time back.

Madan was good in studies. There were a large number of boys in the village of his age group. Out of them Omi was his close friend despite the fact that their personal qualities were at a tangent. Omi never took interest in his studies and used to copy homework from Madan's notebook at the last minute while going to school. The two belonged to different communities, one was from the trading community whereas the other (Omi) belonged to the farming clan; their boys mostly joined the police or military service as a customary profession. Madan was also handsome, tall and healthy and the people of the village particularly the retired ones, from the military service would often joke with his father Hari Ram to send him to the uniformed services. Nature had endowed him with many estimable qualities. He was constitutionally frank and open, detesting every species of falsehood and dishonesty. He was generous even in childhood to the extent that once his father took him to the city and bought him a new pair of shoes. While Madan was sitting alone on a tea shop where his father left him for a while to make other purchases for his grocery shop, he saw one poor boy of his age barefooted, his foot partially bruised. Madan could not see that boy suffering and gave his new shoes to him.

"Where are your new shoes, Madan" Asked Hari Ram on return.

Madan said with tears running down his cheeks, "It was to save a poor boy from absolute destruction in this cold, I parted with your present, not with standing all the values that I had for it."

Hari Ram stood silent at the generosity of his son, his eyes filled with tears. He dismissed Madan with a gentle rebuke advising him to speak to Hari Ram in future before relieving the distressed, in future.

Madan was sober, discreet and pious beyond his age and was praised by all. His close friend Omi on the other hand, as a lad was an 'idle' thoughtless, rattling rascal, disrespectful to his teachers and prone to mischievous frolics. But both teenagers got along well, because Madan had decided to reform him in his company.

Madan was fearless since he had unflinching faith in God that nothing can happen without his wish. Even birth and death are pre-ordained by the God.

One day Omi with three other boys came to Madan's house in the evening and asked for him.

"Madan, we are going to see a 'Ramlila' (an act of Ramayan) in the nearby village Tigri which as you know is about three miles from here. We will leave around 6 PM to be there before it starts. Today is 'Dushera' and last day of Ramlila when Ravana (the demon) shall be killed by lord Rama. We want you to come with us otherwise we will also not go," Said Omi, knowing that Madan will never say no for religious functions.

"OK, I shall come with you. I know you all are scared of going through 'cremation ground' which is adjoining 'Pipalwala Pond' which is astride the track to that village, enroute," said Madan.

Pipal wala pond was known to be haunted by ghosts. As per the stories passed on from generations in village Rajgarh, there were ghosts who lived in that Pipal tree and often troubled people who passed through that area during night. These ghosts as told would sometimes appear as a lamb so to tempt a passerby to grab it. And once some one tried to catch it, this would turn into buffalo. The buffalo then would chase the person up to the village which was at a distance of one mile or till one collapsed enroute, either fell sick or died.

"Do not display your bravado, we can all go without you also," Omi spoke angrily, knowing fully well that Madan can not forego an offer to attend a religious activity and secondly for his close friendship with him.

All the five boys (between the age group of 12 to 14 years) left at 6 PM as per schedule for Tigri village; of course with the permission of their parents which Madan though not the oldest, confirmed from all before departure. Parents were also not worried for their children's security at night since Madan was with them, who was known for his maturity and wisdom beyond his age.

It was month of October, there was enough light till 7.30 PM and the boys made it to that village in good time. The last act of 'Ramlila' began at 8 PM.

"Who is that with ten heads," Asked one of the boys from Madan.

"He is demon Ravana of Lanka. He kidnapped 'Sitaji' wife of lord Rama from 'Panchvati' while they were out in jungle for 14 years exile. He has lost all his sons and other relations in the battle just to fulfill his lust. Today he will also be killed. This will be the victory of 'Dharam' over 'Paap' (Good over evil)", Explained Madan.

"Why did Lord Ram come to jungles that too for 14 years with his brother and wife Sita," Asked the youngest of the boys from Madan who had lurking doubts about the veracity of epic Ramayana.

"Lord Ram was the eldest of the four sons of king 'Dashratha' of Ayodhya, who had three queens: Lord Ram was born to queen Kaushilya, Bharat was born to queen Kekai and Laxman and Shatrughan to queen Sumitra. As per the epic queen Kekai had a 'promise' (vardan) pending with the king Dashratha on account of some good deed performed by the queen and the king was immensely obliged with that. At the time of 'Rajtilak' of Lord Rama to succeed his father king Dashratha who had grown old and wanted to retire, queen Kekai reminded the king of her vardan pending with the king to fulfill. The king agreed and queen Kekai asked her son Bharat to be the king instead of Lord Ram and that Lord Ram be given 14 years exile (vanvas) in the jungles. The king Dashratha had to agree to that since he was morally bound, by his vardan; but soon died with that shock that as per customs and traditions only the eldest of the sons inherit the throne and that what he agreed to was in violation to ethics of kingship," Briefed Madan who had heard Ramayana from his mother.

"But why did queen Kekai asked for 14 years vanvas for Ram," Further queried the boy very innocently.

"Lord Ram was the reincarnation of God Vishnu, who came to earth in form of Avtaar to eradicate ills and sins when these were committed in excess on humanity by the demons that time and the humanity prayed and sought for help from the Almighty. The destiny of Lord Ram was designed like that to go to jungles and eliminate the demon who had created havoc among the saints and general public. Queen Kekai who later regretted her action was also not at fault since she was also influenced by the course of destiny," Further explained Madan.

"What enmity did Ravana have with Lord Ram," Asked the boy promising Madan that to be the last question since the act of Ramlila was about to begin.

"King Ravana of Lanka was a saintly person, but after getting blessings of God through his prayers and bhakti he attained supreme powers of which he became very proud. He also started harassing the people since no one could challenge his power and strength. It was again pre ordained by God to bring an end to tyranny of Ravana's rule, he was made to kidnap Sitaji. Today the final act of Ramlila would show his end," Explained Madan.

The show went on till midnight with lot of fire works to mark the end of Ravana. All the boys were so engrossed in the play that none of them realized how the time passed to midnight. They all left in a jubiliant mood back for their village Rajgarh at about 1 AM. The sticks that they were carrying as a weapon for protection from wild animals enroute were instilling confidence in them.

All the boys were busy discussing the roles played by each artist in the Ramlila while walking fast towards their village. The area was open due to absence of vegetation in the sandy terrain, but the track to the village was clearly visible. The atmosphere at that time of the night was absolutely calm and quiet except the conversation of these boys among themselves, was echoing. All of a sudden there was a loud howling from a group of jackals in the area of Pipalwala pond which was just 500 yards away from these boys; immediately followed by similar response from another group from the area little behind them, which totally terrified the young lads. Jackals and fox are in abundance in desert areas and they are in habit of howling in groups at night which is immediately responded by other groups from different locations in series. All the boys were thinking about the mystery of Pipalwala pond as they were nearing it and mustering courage that this abrupt yell from group of jackals further precipitated the already deep rooted fear in the boys. They all stopped walking and got close to each other almost hugging, seeking some kind of relief from unisom.

All the boys were terribly scared except Madan who was visibly less perturbed not because of the fear of ghosts, who he never believed in, but for the jackals who were known to attack some children particularly at night in groups. The boys were all looking up to Madan for some solution in that acute crises.

"We told you that it is not safe going on this track through Pipalwala pond at night because these ghosts now turned into jackals certainly would kill us," Angrily spoke two boys to Omi.

"There are no ghosts, these are just stories made out by our ancestors for the children to keep them in order. The howl that you have just heard is of the jackals," Madan said.

"No, I do not agree. There are ghosts. Last week my Uncle who died last year at the age of 35 years, appeared in my mother and demanded lot of things. He even threatened that if we failed to meet his requirements he would harm the family," Said one of the boys, trembling, which was agreed to by others also with a nod.

Madan realized that it was difficult to convince these boys about the non-existence of ghosts and unless something was immediately done someone may even collapse because of fear.

"OK, I agree with you that ghosts are there, but they can not kill or harm a person. The birth and death of a human is in the hands of Almighty God, which are pre ordained and no one can alter it," Said Madan in a assuring tone.

"How can you be sure of it," Asked Omi in a subdued voice.

Madan—To convince you all I shall narrate an incident which was told by my mother to me.

"Once there was a young boy who lived in a hired room in one small town, where he used to work as a casual labour in a floor mill, away from his own village. His working time were during day only. One day there was a knock at his door late at night. The boy opened the door and found a ghost standing in front of him. The ghost entered the room, pushing the boy aside. The boy was scared. The ghost told him that he would not harm him if he allowed him to stay in his room and cooked for him daily. The ghost also cautioned the boy not to tell anyone about him or else he would kill him. The boy agreed due to fear of death and both continued living together.

One day the boy asked the ghost who used to be daily out during night and returned early morning, about his employment. The ghost who by then had become little friendly to the boy told him that he went to God 'Dharamraj's darbar (God of maintaining records of human deeds) and he was one of the gatekeepers of the record room at night. The records of all human beings death and birth were kept there. The boy felt little happy and requested the ghost if he could find out as to how long he would live. The ghost readily agreed for the help in order to show his importance and accessibility to such high value records.

The ghost was able to find the age of the boy that night, from one of the clerks working in 'Dharamraj' office on the condition of anonymity; and he looked very happy and boastful when returned in the morning. They boy could guess the outcome and requested for the information. The ghost told that the age of the boy was 72 years, 5 months, 13 days as per the records maintained by Dharamraj on behest of God. Soon on hearing this the boy started crying. The ghost asked the boy the reason for his crying. The boy said that '13' was an unlucky number for him and he would request if it could be deleted or changed to some other number. The ghost pacifying the boy, agreed to help him.

The next night the ghost again approached the same clerk for the change of number '13' to either 12 or 14 or any other number available. The clerk rebuked the ghost and told him the sanctity of the 'Dharamraj' records in which not a single second in age of a human being could be changed by anyone. These were absolutely sacrosanct; not even God would do it once recorded. The ghost next day feeling sorry, told the same to the boy that not a single second change in one's age could be made; not even God would do that. Hearing this the boy picked up a stick, lying in the corner of the room and started beating the ghost; saying that if even God can not kill me before the recorded age, how could you do that. The ghost ran away saving his own life from the boy.

The story gave a lot of confidence to the boys and all got ready to move. Madan, of course told them to watch out for jackals which were plenty in the area. The boys from the villages knew how to deal with the jackals since they had heard of a number of encounters from their elders and knew that jackal was a timid animal. They were only scared of the ghost, fears of which were also shed away on hearing the story from Madan. They all looked confident even while walking through 'Pipalwal pond, ready to attack the jackals with their sticks. Though some of them were still looking at the Pipal tree while passing through that area since stories of ghosts were deeply embedded into their hearts by the villagers.

"We all must learn to pray and trust the God like Madan. See, how bold he looked last night when we all were terrified because of his faith in God," Said one of the boys to Omi when they met the next day.

"Yes, you are right we must try and copy him in his day todays dealings also. See how respectful he is to teachers and other elder people of the village," Said Omi.

The boys of the village started seeking company of Madan including those who were earlier jealous of his popularity because of his behavior and good conduct with all. Even Madan was feeling good seeing some change in the attitudes of these boys. They all studied together, played together. Kabbadi was the popular game which most boys played since it did not cost anything and lot of sandy patches were available as suitable play ground in the village.

It was a 'Diwali' day (festival of lamps and sweets). There were lot of activities in the village. Children were dressed in new clothes, were heading for a congregation near the village temple in the evening. There was a kabbadi match organized by the villagers as a customary ritual on Diwali day with a prize to the winner team. The boys got organized into two different teams as per their 'Mohalas' (segment of village). Omi made one team of his part which included Madan also.

The kabbadi match began at 6 PM in the evening. Both the teams were comparable in strength and physique. Winning of cash prize and a shield from the gram panchayat was treated as a big honour for the winning team and that 'Mohalla'. People were automatically divided in cheering their respective teams during the play. There was lot of excitement and fear of some foul play by an odd person loomed large, hence strict rules were enforced and closely observed.

Both the teams were running neck to neck. Madan and Omi were the key players of their team. Their team was leading by one point and the match was nearing to a close. It was the turn of the opposite team to go in to other side. Ranjit a young boy who was always a rival of Madan captained the opposite team; went in for the final run in which was a deciding point for the win. As he went in, Madan caught him but Ranjit gave a nasty blow on the nose of Madan and got free. It was totally a foul play also declared by the referee. Madan's nose started bleeding and there was suddenly a tension since both the sides came out in open fight. The situation was brought under control and the matter was left to be decided the next day by the gram panchayat. Both the teams were claiming the victory so were the villagers depending upon their alliances.

"Why did you hit Madan intentionally," Asked the Sarpanch of the village panchayat from Ranjit.

"NO, I did not hit him, it was accidental. The last point should be awarded to our team and match be declared drawn," Replied Ranjit who was known to be a mischief monger in the village.

The panchayat found Ranjit guilty of the offence and decided to pass a judgement of one year ban on Ranjit in playing kabbadi matches. The panchayat wanted to hear Madan's version also to complete the proceedings, though both the sides were amply clear and convinced of the mischief on part of Ranjit and were feeling bad for Madan, who was so nice and a sober boy.

"We have found Ranjit guilty beyond any doubt. He deliberately hit you with a pre design, which has caused you a severe injury. We want to disqualify him for one year for playing kabbadi matches. Do you wish to say anything," Asked the panchayat from Madan.

"I do not agree with the opinion of the panchayat. Ranjit did not hit me. It was by accident that I fell on him and his hand struck my nose which started bleeding. He is a promising player of kabbadi of our school and village team and should not be disqualified," Said Madan, in all humility.

"Are you under threat or duress from someone," Asked the Sarpanch who was surprised to hear Madan's version who had been deliberately wronged by Ranjit.

"No, I am not under any pressure nor I am scared of anyone. I am following my mother's teachings to me of benevolence and love for all. For never in this world does hatred ceased by hatred; hatred ceases by love and let a man overcome anger by kindness and evil by good," Spoke Madan, hypnotizing the entire gathering with his eloquence and wisdom.

"We are pround of you my son. I wish other boys of this village also learn something from you which will be useful to them throughout their lives," Said the Sarpanch of the village, patting Madan's back in praise. Ranjit who was sitting closely also got up with folded hands and confessed to the panchayat. He hugged Madan and begged for a pardon for his crime. Lala Hari Ram was also proud of his son Madan who had raised his stature high in the village by his extra ordinary disposition and conduct that day.

Time passed, Madan had reached his 8th class in the school. Omi who in the company of Madan had improved a little and had also reached 8th standard. The parents of Omi openly attributed the change in their son to the good company of Madan.

Shanti, the mother of Madan was particularly keen to see her son do well in life. One day a famous saint came to the village temple. Lot of people were seeking his blessings and asking about their future. The news reached Shanti also who took Madan to the saint and asked about his future.

"Is he your son," Asked the saint smiling.

"Yes Baba, he is my only son after three daughters. I am concerned about his future," Said Shanti.

"Do not worry about his future. God has already planned it for him. He will one day bacome a man of fame and repute," Told the saint.

Shanti returned home happily and shared the prophecy made by the saint with her husband who though did not believe much in such predictions.

Janmashtmi (festival of Lord Krishna's birth) was being celebrated in the village temple as an yearly ritual. Village panchayat was arranging ceremony. One young boy from the village based on his overall performance used to be nominated to represent Lord Krishna. There was always a competition among young boys for this nomination but this year, Madan's name was unanimously agreed to by all for this prestigious role. Lala Hari Ram and his wife were very happy hearing their son being nominated that year to represent Lord Krishna which was considered an implicit blessing of the God.

The Sarpanch of the village led the choir, danced along with others of all castes and they were totally absorbed in the performance. All present imagined themselves to be true disciples of Lord Krishna. The worshippers were so elated with the feeling of universal love and joy that they fouled on some religious decorum. At night when Lord Krishna was born one 'conch' was sounded. In India where all else is usually unpunctuated, the hour of the birth of Lord Krishna is chronometrically observed. The noise of the people talking excitedly became louder and louder. The normal tension created by racial prejudice in the village had been lessened by the atmosphere created in that religious function.

As Madan appeared as Lord Krishna on the dais people started touching his feet and made offerings to the Lord depending upon their finances. Of course complete offerings were being collected by the poojari (*priest*) immediately and taken in his charge. The poojari was sitting on a mat next to Madan and a brass platter of coins lay near him. But for Madan who was the hero of that day it was an honour and a privilege to be nominated to represent Lord Krishna.

Madan after having passed his 8th class joined a government high school in a nearby town, about three kms from Rajgarh. He used to go walking to the school along with two other boys of the same village who were also studying with him.

Madan was good in studies and in due course he got promoted to 10th class at the age of 15 years. Hari Ram was slightly worried looking for matches for his two grown up daughters. Though suitable boys were available but their dowry demand was very high which Hari Ram was not in a position to meet. Shanti, mother of Madan used to remain slightly ill and on the top of it the expenses of the marriage of two daughters further aggravated her condition. Hari Ram also used to remain slightly depressed and worried.

"What is wrong with you, Papa, you do not seem to be as happy as you used to be," Asked Madan.

"No son there is nothing to worry, I am thinking how to organize marriage of your both the sisters. There are two brothers in a good family but their dowry demand is slightly high which we can not meet," Told Hari Ram.

"How much is that ? Why can't we sell our one bigha of land which is just lying like that and marry of both the sisters well," Suggested Madan.

"No, as it is, we do not have much property in this village and I have to leave something for you also to survive on, after we left," Said Hari Ram.

"Do not worry about me Papa, I shall take care of myself, you sell that land and marry both my sisters," Said Madan.

Hari Ram agreed to the suggestion of the young son who had finished his education, passed matriculation. Both the girls were married off well. Time went by and Hari Ram's wife Shanti who used to be ill, died after six months of their daughters marriage. Both male members were only left in the family ie. the father and the son. The house was managed by the married girls in rotation. Madan took on the business of his father and Hari Ram who had gone old started relaxing, a partially retired life.

"Papa, you are looking very happy today, What is the matter? Whose letter is that you are carrying in hand," Enquired Madan.

"There is good news. Lakshmi has been blessed with a son and they have invited us also to attend the 'Namkaran' ceremony," Told Hari Ram.

"What an excellent news! I must inform everyone around, particularly Dadi Kamla who has been enquiring about it everyday, since Lakshmi was expecting," Said Madan.

"Yes you may do that. But I do not know whom to send to this function since I am not too well to travel that long and you can not leave the business," Hari Ram said.

"Why can't I go ? I shall go to Tinsukhia. Lakshmi would be expecting me. The business can be looked after by you. Papa, for a few days," Madan replied.

Hari Ram was not keen to send Madan again on that route lest should he again remember his past life and the troubles start all over again. Though Madan had grown matured at the age of about 16 years and took full care of his father's small business and other management of the house.

Madan insisted, "I shall only go father, I will not stay longer there since I know you need me here also."

"OK, if you insist then go, but take care of yourself, return soon, I shall miss you here, now that your mother is also no more to give me company," Very hesitatingly agreed Hari Ram, who demurred and prayed for Madan's well being.

Madan boarded the same Tinsukhia Mail from New Delhi Railway station in which he had already travelled once. It was a different kind of experience for Madan now that he was grown up, educated and travelling alone, all by himself. He had his berth reserved in III Tier.

"Where are you going to," Asked an old man who was on the adjoining berth.

"I am going to Tinsukhia to attend a 'Namkaran' ceremony. My eldest sister who lives there with her family has been blessed with a son," Replied Madan.

"Where are you going Uncle," Asked Madan.

"I am going up to Dibrugarh, a city very close to Tinsukhia. I shall also get down at Tinsukhia. My two sons are in business there and have almost settled there only. I am just going to spend sometime with them, may be just a month or so," Replied the old man.

"What business are your sons in, Uncle," Asked Madan again.

"One is in trading, has his cloth show room and the other one who is younger of the two, deals in sale of 'ginger', which is sold mostly in Delhi market," Said the old man.

"What do you do for your living, my son," Asked the old man.

"We have a small shop of kiryana (grocery) in our village. My father used to look after it. Now that he has gone old and generally retired, I am running it," Told Madan.

"How much can you earn from such a small shop? It may not even meet your house hold expenses also? A young man like you should think of something better rather than just sticking to such outdated business," Advised the old man.

"Yes Uncle you are right, but we have no finance to increase this business or start a new venture in the village. In any case there is no scope for a new venture there," Said Madan.

The two kept on talking off and on, till they went to sleep that night. The train had slowed down, it was about 4.30 AM in the morning. Madan all of a sudden got up and voluntarily walked up to the gate of the train which had just come to a halt. It was Rangiya railway station but Madan remembered nothing and again went to his berth and slept.

The train was on time at Tinsukhia railway station. Navrang had come to take Madan at the station.

“How was the journey,” Asked Navrang doubting some kind of relapse of the earlier episode at Rangiya.

“It was nice, there was a good company of one old man who has also come to Tinsukhia to meet his sons who are settled at Dibringarh,” Replied Madan.

There were lot of activities at Laksmi’s house. People were making arrangement for the ‘Namkaran’ ceremony which was next day. Lakshmi was also worried about Madan since he had once again passed through Rangiya. But Navrang informed her of all being well with Madan. It was the feast day too where lot of people had gathered. Some of them who knew Madan wanted to know about his well being.

After attending the ceremony Madan did not stay long despite request from Laksmi and her husband since he was obsessed with the idea of doing some new business at Rajgarh as advised by the old man in the train.

Madan happily returned to Rajgarh. He returned within a week only. His father Hari Ram was very happy to see Madan back hale and hearty since he also had apprehensions of the repeat of the episode of his re incarnation.

“How are everyone at Tinsukhia,” Asked Hari Ram. “All are fine and were very happy with the addition in the family. The child of Lakshmi is very cute and handsome," Said Madan.

"That is nice. Now that you are back, take care of the shop which was generally closed in your absence," Said Hari Ram.

"Papa, I wanted to talk to you regarding change of business since we are not getting much from the shop," Informed Madan.

"What business do you want to start in this village which affords no viability and where are the finances to start anything," Asked Hari Ram.

"Though Dada Ram Chandar is keen to purchase our shop, but we will not do that since you are emotionally attached to it being our inheritance. I shall instead take some loan from the bank in Sikar. Narender from our village who is a clerk there has promised to help me in this," Informed Madan.

"How much can you get from the bank? And what business do you have in mind to run with such a meager amount," Asked Hari Ram.

"Papa, I shall get about Rupees ten thousands as loan for which we shall have to mortgage our shop to the bank as a security," Told Madan.

Hari Ram—No, I can not give my shop to the bank which is so dear to me like my family. It has seen me through during difficult times. I can not part with it. Sorry you better plan something else.

Madan—Papa the shop will remain with us only and you can keep it running. Once we pay back the loan, it will be released back to us. This will be a paper transaction only.

"OK, what business do you wish to start with this amount," Asked Hari Ram.

Madan—Since the amount is very small, I wish to start fodder business since there have been a famine in the area and every farmer is looking for fodder for the cattles, I shall bring it from UP and store in our plot and sell it at reasonable profit. There is no risk involved in it, what so ever.

Hari Ram—OK, go ahead, but I shall not close my shop.

Having got the permission from his father Madan got in touch with Narender who was a bank employee in Sikar from Rajgarh only. Madan had taken all the papers of the shop for mortgage as required by the bank. With little running around, Madan got rupees ten thousands as loan from the bank. He got in touch with fodders dealers in UP and his business picked up well. Madan was making good profit and with his rapport they started giving him fodder on credit also. Madan was not only catering for the needs of Rajgarh village but a number of adjoining villages also.

His business was doing extremely well. Within six months of its comencement, he had a stock of fodder approximately of rupees thirty thousands with him which he could manage on credit. Everyone was very happy see Madan do well.

It was about 9 PM in the evening, someone came running, shouting Madan, Madan your fodder stock has caught fire and it is profusely burning. Madan ran out of the house and with the help of the villagers he started extinguishing the fire, but all in vain. Every bit of dry fodder was burning like kerosene oil. Everything disappeared in just few moments. Hari Ram could not stand this shock and died of heart attack. Madan was left alone, with one of his sisters to look after him and lot of money to be paid back to people, which Madan did not have. It was as if hell fell on Madan.

His every bit of happiness got ruined. He was left with nothing since the shop was also mortgaged to the bank and it was auctioned by the bank to liquidate the loan. Madan had the least inkling of that impending disaster caused by fire. People even thought he was victim of well calculated conspiracy since some boys, his contemporaries were jealous of Madan flourishing in the business. The fire in his stock yard was not accidental, but lit by someone as part of ill design, they thought. Madan could hardly manage his affairs in the village. One day his neighbour, another old man Dhanpat Rai of Madan's cast took pity on his promising young man and asked him to go to Delhi to one of his distant relations who was a big businessman there; though he had not been in touch with him for a long time. Madan was happy at the new prospect but sad to leave his house. He kept thinking about one time his happy family including so loving parents, sisters, the whole night. The very idea of leaving the village was terribly troubling him. Though he had passed through Delhi, but he was totally unaware of its vast layout including the behaviour and conduct of people there. These thoughts did not let Madan sleep the whole night. Tormenting thoughts crowded upon him. He was regretting having started the fodder business which made him lose his father and landed him in such a state. He felt guilty as if he had committed enormous sin. It was terrible night, never had such situation ever risen in his life time. Once happy family got ruined with one stroke. Man's politic and scheme are inconsequential in the over all plan of nature. Madan was trying to derive solace and strength from her mother's old advice, "In case misfortune comes, one should accept it stoically without angry complaint or sentimental self pity. Tribulations and sufferings can not become permanent feature in one's life. Dark night must be succeeded by a bright night."

It was summer night. Madan was lying on the charpoy out in open, looking at the sky. The moon was surrounded by a cluster of twinkling stars, but that sight had no joy for Madan that night. He was comparing himself with the stars breaking away abruptly from the cluster and vanishing once for all in the horizon. The horror of the universe and its smallness were haunting him. Madan took gloomy view of life that night for he felt miserable and helpless and nothing to fall back upon. The whole night Madan was brooding and talking to himself and crying incessantly. At times he would get up and go around (the compound of the house), look at the 'chullah' (an earthern fire place to cook food) of his late mother where she used to cook, surrounded and chased by the children for their turn for the food. Filled with unbearable sobs, he would come out to peep into the street to find it deserted except the 'yell' of a chowkidar' (night guard) at a distance, detailed by the gram panchayat to take rounds in the streets at night as a security arrangements particularly against thefts.

It was around 4 AM, early in the morning. Madan was still lying on his chorpoy. His faith in the God was unflinching. In order to get some solace he started praying and in that course went to sleep. His late mother Shanti appeared in his dream and she asked Madan not to cry and follow her. Madan accompanied her on foot on a road which was frightening. No mile stones marked its progress. No trees grew along it. No birds were chirping around. No twists, no turns or hairpin bends obscured their clear view up to a long distance. Soon a 'Saint' appeared in front of them. Shanti touched his feet and Madan too followed her. She asked about the future of Madan from the Saint. The Saint told Madan not to lose his moorings and faith in God and that it was a test of time and all would be well with the blessings of Almighty in due course. The Saint and his mother Shanti disappeared and Madan suddenly got up to find it to be 5 AM, the time to start preparing for his departure.

"Madan it is time now to get up and get ready since bus leaves at 7 AM for Sikar which is the only private bus, once a day," Informed his friend Omi.

"Yes, I am already awake and ready. Let us go. It is already 6.15 AM," Said Madan.

Omi his best friend had brought some packed food for Madan which his mother had cooked for him. There was a big gathering of villagers out side Madan's house who had come to see him off. Everyone was feeling utterly sad on the way the misfortunes fell on this one time happy family and this promising young boy in particular. They all were in tears. The love and affection of people of village who are so closely and deeply rooted together, was visible.

"Madan take this twenty ruppes; you will need it in Delhi where you know none and will take time to settle down," Said Omi his friend on the quiet.

"Thank you for this help and kind gesture, very hesitatingly accepting money," Madan said. "This is a loan to me, I shall return it as soon as possible," Further added Madan.

Madan left Rajgarh empty handed, leaving everyone in the village in tears, and headed for Delhi to try his luck. It appeared he was fated to involve himself in endless troubles.

IV

Sikar was not a very new place for Madan since he used to come here for his business. But what was new and moving, were the circumstances under which Madan was leaving the place. Having bought his railway ticket, he boarded the train, generally oblivious of his surroundings in the compartment. The memory of his house, family and the village were haunting him. There were varying thoughts good and bad coming to his mind. His only hope was now the Almighty.

The train steamed off at 10 AM as per schedule. The compartment was full of passengers now. The rush in the compartment did not bother Madan, who by then had been squeezed in the corner by the crowd. He was giving an appearance of half asleep and when asked to shift by the passengers to accommodate themselves, he just did not bother if there was still a space to shift nor did he feel like looking at anyone.

Madan was suddenly awakened when he heard a blind man, escorted by his small son, singing in that compartment and begging. This shook Madan's conscience that there were people who were more miserable than him in life and the dignity of labour was important. This gave some morale boosting and encouragement to Madan, who then became little alert and normal.

The train reached Delhi Railway station at 5 PM. Madan was totally new to the place and was looking totally lost. He however followed the co-passengers to the exit.

"Excuse me bhai shab, I want to go to Tri Nagar, how do I go? can you please tell", Asked Madan from a coolie.

"Yes, go to the next chowk (crossroads), on the left, there is a local bus stand, ask people the number of the bus going to Tri Nagar," Guided the coolie.

Madan walked up to the chowk and saw lot of local buses parked there and waiting to leave. Lot of people were purchasing tickets from the window.

"Which bus will go to Tri Nagar, bhai shab," Gently asked Madan from the man sitting on the enquiring counter and also selling tickets."

What do you think I am doing? Take out four annas and take a ticket for Tri Nagar. This bus No 42 will go there," Curtly spoke the man.

Madan purchased a ticked and boarded the bus for Tri Nagar. It was about 6 PM when the bus started for Tri Nagar. Madan was getting worried and scared as the sun was coming close to setting in since he was a stranger and secondly he did not know the location of the business man's house in Tri Nagar, where he was referred to. As the bus was passing through the busy streets of Delhi where lights were getting lit, his fears were compounding, lot of thoughts including cursing the self were coming to his mind.

The bus reached Tri Nagar at 7 PM. Madan also got down, but did not know which direction to go. He took out a small piece of paper from his pocket and asked a passerby for that address.

"Bhai shab can you please tell me this address, I am totally new to this city," Very politely asked Madan showing the slip to a passerby.

"Yes, it is straight and very close, you can walk up to that place, it will just take five minutes from here. Ask for Lala Ganpat Ram's kothi, anyone will tell you," Briefed that man.

"Thank you, sir, I shall find it now," Madan said leaving that place.

It was getting dark. Madan was moving in correct direction on the road towards Lala Ganpat Ram's kothi. As he reached a tri junction, he noticed a big house, with high boundary walls and big iron gate. There was one darban (guard) also in khaki dress with a stick in his hand. Madan thought it had to be the house he was looking for and he having crossed the road reached the gate of the house.

"Who is there," Shouted the guard.

"I am Madan, have come from Rajgarh village in Sikar District of Rajasthan. I want to meet Seth Ganpat Ram ji. One of his relations has sent me here," Said Madan.

"Sorry, Lala ji is no more. He died last month. Only his two sons live here. Gobind the eldest son of late lalaji now looks after his business." Told the guard.

"Can I meet him now," Asked Madan from the guard.

"No, not now, it is too late. You can come in the morning at 8 AM. I shall let you meet him; that is the time he goes for his work," Told the guard.

"I have no where to go. I know none here in Delhi, what should I do? Can you please help me?", Requested Madan.

"OK since I am also from Rajasthan and you appear very simple and innocent, I shall suggest you sleep in this park, adjoining this house. It is quite open and pleasant," Advised the guard.

"Will I be allowed to sleep there," Asked Madan.

The guard, "Yes, Yes, I am here in case of any problem. The chowkidar there knows me. Tell him that you are my guest, my name is Chandgi Ram."

Madan went to the park. There were a few people still sitting there in the lawn. Some children were also playing near the main lights in the park. Madan went around the park and found one suitable place in open for himself to spend the night. There was plenty of water available and Madan had no problem in the night except the fear of unknown, ie his destiny, his luck. It was 7.30 AM Madan had finished his bath and normal routine for the day and reached the gate around 8 AM.

"Namaste Bhai shab, I have come," Told Madan to the guard, Chandgi Ram, who was also preparing to leave since he was on night shift.

"Good that you have come, I was waiting for you only otherwise I leave around 8 AM soon after chhotta Lalaji leaves for office," Replied Chandgi Ram, the guard.

"Come, the car is about to start the chhota Lalaji has already got in, stand near me. When the car stops I will tell lalaji about you and then you say Namaste to him and ask for a job giving reference of that man who sent you here," Briefed Chandgi Ram.

The car started, the new guard opened the gate, Chandgi Ram who appeared to be well known to Lalaji's family being one of the oldest employees, saluted at the gate. The car stopped, the lala pulled down the window pane, and Chandagi Ram informed him about the boy standing next to him.

"Yes, where have you come from? And what do you want," Asked lala from Madan.

"Namaste Sahib, I have been sent by Danpat Rai from village Rajgarh. I am looking for some employment. I am very poor, no where to go. I shall request you to give me some job," Pleaded Madan.

"I don't know any Danpat Rai. My father who is no more may have known him. Also I have no job for you, sorry," The lala replied and went off.

Madan could not help bursting into tears since this was only the hope for him. Lala flatly refused. There was total black out for Madan as if the world has come to an end for him. He sat down weeping. Chandgi Ram too was moved by seeing the pathetic condition of the boy and his total helplessness.

"Do not worry Madan, come with me, I am a very small person but have been in Delhi for almost 15 years, I shall do something for you," Encouraged Chandgi Ram.

Hearing this Madan got up and touched Chandgi Ram's feet." You are God sent for me at this critical juncture. May God give you all the happiness in life," Said Madan.

Chandgi Ram used to live in a very small room in village Shamli, adjoining Tri Nagar. He took Madan with him to his room. He told Madan to rest there and he would try and fix some job for him since he knew a few people particularly from Rajasthan, now working in Delhi. We can not force vital solution, every problem must bide time.

Chandgi Ram tried, went around, met known people to fix some job for Madan, but it did not work. Chandgi Ram was finding it difficult to feed, two persons on his meager salary. Though Madan also had about forty rupees with him in person to help Chandgi Ram in running the kitchen but Chandgi would not take it.

One day Chandgi Ram got a call from his village in Rajasthan that his mother was very ill and he was required to reach there the soonest. Chandgi Ram managed to leave for a few days. As a stop gap arrangement Chandgi Ram fixed Madan as a casual worker with a building contractor in Tri Nagar where there was a construction work of a government school. Chandgi Ram told Madan to do that work to meet his kitchen expenses till he returned and then he would find a suitable job for him; and he left that evening for his village.

Madan not aware of the kind of work he would be employed on by the contractor, reached Tri Nagar at the construction site at about 8 AM, the next day.

"Where can I meet the building contractor," Asked Madan from a labourer who was carrying bricks and putting close to the mason, from the dump.

"He would come around 9 AM. That is his office in the small room in that corner," Replied the labourer, not even bothering to look at Madan.

Madan waited at the site for the contractor. He went around the site looking for and guessing as to what kind of work he could be employed on by the contractor. Since he could find only labourers and masons busy in carrying construction matrial on the second floor and in the construction of the building respectively, he could really identify no work for self since he thought to be educated and expected to be assigned some supervisory or clerical jobs.

"He is the contractor, dressed in blue shirt and trouser," Told the same labourer whom Madan had asked initially." Thank you, I will meet him," Replied Madan and went to the contractor to meet.

"Namaste Sir, I have been sent by Chandgi Ram to you for some job," Said Madan very humbly.

Looking at Madan, who appeared very delicate and neat and clean, the contractor asked Madan as to what job he could do since his work involved totally physical labour. Madan was shocked to hear that since he was not prepared mentally and physically for such a laborious and physically tough job which he had never done in his life.

"Do not you have some supervisory job or office job, I am metric pass," Asked Madan from the contractor.

"I am not a very big contractor. The supervisory and office work I do myself. I can't afford to create a separate infra structure for this small work," Apprised the contractor smiling. "I pay only one rupee daily to each labourer," Further said the contractor.

Madan did not know what to decide and say. He was without any work in Delhi for a number of days. He was on his own in the absence of Chandgi Ram, to fend for self. Since he was new in Delhi and nowhere to go for help, Madan opted for any job the contractor could find for him. He was not destitute of virtues but he realized that his stars were unfavourable.

The contractor asked his senior, old looking mason to employ the boy. Madan, on some suitable work and accordingly Madan started working on the site of the construction.

Chandgi Ram who had gone only for a few days had to delay his return longer, since he lost his mother and was to return only after performing all the rituals (Teherva). Madan had no choice but to continue working with the contractor to earn his living despite he found himself physically and mentally incapable of such a tough labour. He used to get so tired sometimes, carrying construction material to the second floor that soon on return to his room in the evening, he would straight away go to sleep without even taking his evening meals. His clothes had also got dirty and torn in that job. Since he did not know cooking, he would eat all his meals outside from a local market. He even did not find time to wash his clothes regularly. He abhorred the process, but had no alternative to subsist on.

Madan kept cursing his luck but never lost faith in the Almighty. Sometimes he cried at night, lying on his bed, on his plight and remembering his once happy family. His exposure in the public was adding to his experience to face life. One day Madan had woken up at night to escape from a familiar recurrent dream in which policeman approached him with snicking scissors, wanting to hack off his hair. They did it in Tri Nagar market of Delhi that day to a pick pocket boy, branded him so that everybody would know him for what he was and policeman on beat would have no problem identifying whom to harass. Madan always noticed him thereafter when he went for work, the boy with forcibly shaved head.

Chandgi Ram returned that evening and was troubled to see Madan in that state. He sympathized with

Madan and gave him all the encouragement that God would help him and that he would look for a suitable job soon for Madan fitting his conditions; even asked Madan to stop working with the building contractor and take rest in the room, till a suitable job was found for him. Madan had yet not got over the shock of tragedy of fire and sudden loss of his loving and caring father. He was in total remoarse.

Two days passed after return, Chandgi Ram could not find any job for Madan. However on third day, Chandgi Ram remembered of a scrap dealer Harlal who he thought could employ Madan. He took Madan the next day to the scrap dealer in Uttam Nagar.

"Namaste Harlal," Said Chandgi Ram.

"What a pleasant surprise to see you here Chandgi," Replied Harlal.

"Yes, I have come here to you for a very special favour and I am sure you will not refuse," Said Chandgi Ram.

Harlal—Tell me what is it about. I will do anything for you which is within my reach.

Chandgi—This boy is from Rajasthan, from a poor family but educated. He is in urgent need of some job. I think you can employ him here in your stock yard. I shall stand security for his good conduct.

Harlal—Come boy, what is your name and up to what class have you studied?

Madan—I am metric pass, my name is Madan. I will do anything with sincerity and honesty.

Harlal—OK, I shall keep you as a supervisor to keep count of transaction in the stock yard. You can live in this tinned hut. I shall pay you rupees fifty per month. To others, I just pay thirty rupees each.

"I am grateful to you. You will not find any fault with my work," Said Madan.

Chandgi Ram after adjusting Madan left for his room. He gave his contact number and address to Madan in case he needed any of his help later.

Madan settled himself in the hut. His only aim now was not his comforts but to do well and establish in the job. He would get up early morning, get ready, sweep the area around the gate and office of the stock yard and light aggarbatti. This impressed Harlal the owner also. The place which used to give untidy look, became worth sitting and spending some time. Harlal's business also started doing well. He attributed his progress to Madan's hard work and sincerity. Harlal increased his pay from Rupees fifty to seventy five and gave him complete responsibility of his stock yard office to handle. Madan was intelligent and shrewd and soon learned to handle this business in Tri Nagar.

Harlal was very happy with Madan, who had proved his devotion and honesty beyond doubt. Harlal started sending Madan to Banks to deposit cash etc and even at times Madan was asked to do his personal work at Harlal's house. Harlal's wife also started liking this boy for his good conduct and sincerity. Madan had made a place for himself in Harlal's business and in the surrounding area; people now knew Madan as much as Harlal. Madan made himself indispensable to Harlal and he was accepted by him as a family member.

Time went by; five years passed for Madan working with Harlal. Madan was now about 24 years of age. He had earned and deposited around rupees five thousand. Madan was now planning to start his own small business, of-course with the permission of Harlal who and his family by now had started treating Madan as their family member.

"Babu ji, with your permission and if you do not mind may I ask you for an advice," Very politely submitted Madan.

"Yes, Madan, why not, please go ahead, tell me what you want, I shall be too glad to be of any help to you," Enthusiastically replied Harlal.

Madan—You have been very kind to me, like my own father. Without your help and kindness probably I would have ceased to exist. I can not muster enough strength and courage to tell you about what I have in mind. I think I will tell you sometimes later.

Harlal—No Madan, if you treat me like your own father then don't hesitate. A father is meant to listen to his children good or bad, please go ahead, ask my frankly what you have in mind.

Madan—Babu ji, since I have some money now, saved out of my pay; I was thinking, if I could with your guidance and blessings, start a small business of my own.

Harlal—Oh! my son I am so happy to hear this from you. In fact we in the family were also thinking that it was now time that you started some of your own business. You are so promising, educated and devoted. Such salaried work is meant for lethargic and non-intellectuals and not for people like you.

"What business have you thought of and where," Asked Harlal.

"There is a small place measuring around 150 yards in our market of Tri Nagar for sale. The owner is asking for rupees fifteen hundred for it. If I purchase it and open a small 'khoka' (small wooden frame) and start something in that," Explained Madan to Harlal.

"It will be excellent. I know that place, it is very nicely located on the road and has lot of future as the market develops," Said Harlal.

"But what business do you wish to start," Further asked Harlal.

Madan—I want to start a 'Paan shop' in that, which I think has a market.

Harlal—How much money do you have? I have something better to advise you in which you have knowledge and interest also.

Madan—I have total of about five thousands rupees, of which rupees fifteen hundred will go for the land, another two hundred for the shop. Say, I shall be left with about three thousand rupees for the business.

"That is good amount. We will start another scrap business for you and make that as stock yard. This business is fast increasing and I alone can not handle this. People from other areas are thinking to come to our area in this business seeing us progressing. Before that happens let us start our own here," Said Harlal.

The proposal was finally approved and Madan made a small 'khoka' in that plot and started his business. The old contacts and particularly the conduct and excellent dealings of Madan while working with Harlal paid him well. Madan progressed a lot; of course Harlal was still helping him by giving some business to Madan in addition to what Madan managed own his own. Within two years Madan became a known person in scrap business around Tri Nagar area and other localities of Delhi. He made a proper office for himself. Now Madan was past 26 years of age and appropriate time for him to establish his own family also. Probably need for money was immediate incentive for Madan to start a new venture and it proved financially very remunerative. Business was always an obsession with him. The secret of success as per Madan was constancy of purpose.

Harlal was also from the same community of traders (ie Banias) as was Madan. The family of Harlal had developed tremendous liking for Madan for his all the good traits. Harlal's wife Kunti used to praise Madan a lot. Harlal had one daughter and two sons, the daughter was the eldest who had finished her matric and now was just helping her mother in the house hold.

Madan was tall, strikingly handsome, bold, very inquisitive and progressive. He became popular in Harlal's family chiefly because of his good habits. He treated that family like his own and emotionally shared their feelings. This conduct of Madan vindicated his value and merit with Reena also, the daughter of Harlal who had attained a marriageable age.

Reena was also an extremely beautiful girl, who was well groomed with all the social values. She was not only beautiful but also gentle and noble. She was in every way equal to Madan. She was adorned with all the charms, innocence, modesty and tenderness, breathing sweetness from her rosy lips and darting brightness from her sparkling eyes. She was educated directly under the supervision of her mother, who was a lady of great discretion. Reena overall was a very well bred child.

Madan and Reena had started liking each other. But the social ethos and customs did not permit them to show their infatuation in public. Reena was fond of nature. She had kept a parrot which was presented to her by her aunt. One day the bird managed to cut its string from its leg and flew away. It perched itself on a bough at some distance. Reena screamed so loudly that Madan who was also present that day in their house, reached the branch, where the bird perched, the branch broke and Madan fell in a ditch below. Seeing Madan in danger Reena extended her helping hand and helped Madan get out of the ditch. This incident made a very favourable impression on each other and further brought them closer.

Madan and Reena started finding some time in private to converse when ever Madan visited their house; though the conversation was limited to asking each other well being only. In due course Reena even started talking to Madan in the presence of her brothers. One day Reena and Madan were talking outside the house on the gate that Kunti, mother of Reena noticed them through a window of the house. She was surprised at the extent of her daughter's physical ease with Madan since Kunti always thought her daughter to be dumb founded when it came to talking to boys. She was happily surprised that her child seemed to have a sub world that excluded her entirely. A tactile world of smile that her mother had not part in. Madan standing outside the gate, facing the house, caught Kunti's gaze. He was terribly shaken being caught offguard. He immediately moved away, all sorts of thoughts coming to his mind as to what would Kunti, father like Harlal think of him when told about the conversation. Madan was well aware of reactions from orthodox families on such incidents. He decided not to visit Harlal's house unless called for.

"Now that Reena has grown up and is now 18 years of age, we must look for a suitable boy for her," Said Kunti to Harlal.

"Yes, I was also thinking about it. What is you opinion about our Madan for our daughter Reena. He is handsome, educated, well mannered and from our community only. Now his business is also doing very well, people respect him in the area," Told Harlal.

"You have said exactly what I was about to say," Excitedly said Kunti.

"OK, I will talk to Madan tomorrow when I visit him in his office," Said Harlal.

Next day Harlal went to Madan's stock yard where Madan had made a good office. Madan's business had progressed well and he was financially getting sound. Harlal was fully convinced about the eligibility of Madan for his daughter Reena who was also pious, religious and very homely girl.

"Come, Babu ji, nice you come otherwise I was thinking to come to your office for some advice," Said Madan seeing Harlal entering his office.

"Yes, what advice you need from this old man? You are doing so well that I may even need advice from you someday," Said Harlal laughingly.

"Babu ji, I want to establish a small factory here alongside, for making packing material for various items like radios, glass items and other delicate items. There is tremendous market for it here. Dealers keep asking me to start this manufacture," Told Madan.

"Excellent son, go ahead. Don's worry about anything, I shall also help you," Said Harlal.

"What is that you have come here for, Babu ji," Very respectfully asked Madan from Harlal.

"Nothing son, it was just like that we remembered of you and I thought I look you up and your business on my way to the office," Said Harlal.

Harlal did not find it appropriate to mention about his daughters marriage proposal to Madan since the young man was already mentally occupied with a new business project. Harlal came back home and told about it to his wife Kunti, who of course was waiting for a good news, as mother get more excited on their daughters marriage proposals.

Madan with the help of some loan from the bank and the money that he had earned, established a factory of manufacturing packing material. Harlal very actively helped Madan in this project and even offered some financial help to which Madan very humbly declined and instead got loan from the bank.

This factory of Madan also picked up very fast just within one year he had become a business man with a trade mark in making Packing material. Though very young in age, just about 27 years, but had earned lot of respect and place in the business community.

Reena was now 19 years of age. Harlal and his wife once again decided to approach Madan for their daughter. Though Madan was very frequently visiting Harlal house since he had special attachment with this family and Reena and a sense of obligation for them. Harlal decided to call Madan for tea on Sunday where he planned to propose to Madan. Madan was highly excited to be formally called for tea. He had the inclination of the proposal from Reena. Madan dressed up in best clothes and reached Harlal's house well on time.

"Welcome son, nice to see you feel free from the business for some time at least, said Kunti," Harlal's wife in kind of an appreciation for Madan.

"Yes, Aunty, it is nice to be at home like this for a change," Replied Madan.

All sat down. Normal conversation carried on. Reena was preparing tea and Kunti had prepared some palak pakoras and sweet dishes for Madan. Everyone enjoyed tea and the conversation. Almost two hours had passed and it was time for Madan to leave.

"Son, before you leave I wanted to take your views on your future plans on your marriage. Now that you are well settled in business and is now the time for you to get married," Asked Harlal.

"Yes, babuji I also think so," Said Madan, very shyly.

"Do you have any girl in mind," Again asked Harlal.

"Not as yet, I have left every thing on you about my marriage also. Whatever you will do for me has to be in my interest," Said Madan.

"Son, we were thinking if our daughter Reena will suit you," Said Harlal.

Madan got up and touched Harlal's feet and said, "It shall be my good luck if I can establish such relation in your family."

The engagement and then marriage of Reena and Madan took place. It was wonderful gathering during that marriage. Madan had called lot of people from his village Rajgarh including his three sisters. All were extremely happy to see Madan doing so well within six-seven years and had become so rich.

Life went on. Madan's business further flourished and he established another factory at Rajauri garden. His indomitable courage saw him through the ordeal and he rose to become one of the renowned industrialists.

Madan had arrived in Delhi with his disarming simplicity, integrity and sense of mission and purpose. He became a role model for others in that field. The sense of self satisfaction of complacency resulted from the immense stride that Madan had taken in industrial field. He attributed all the prosperity to God's blessings and his untiring hard work.

Madan was blessed with a son after two years of his marriage, but as ill luck would have it, the child died after four days of his birth. It was indeed a big shock to both Reena and Madan. Madan's Rajouri project was doing extremely well and he started a subsidiary project of the same at Calcutta. God was very kind to Madan and he was blessed with yet another son after a gap of about eight years, with this the only worry that was troubling Madan for a child also got over.

"Madan, I was thinking that it is time we shifted to a bigger house in a good locality. We can afford it now," Said Reena.

"OK, I shall start looking for one. It will be better if we shift to Rajouri Garden area close to our factories. This will help me save that much time of travel," Replied Madan.

It was 1965 and the country was going to war with Pakistan. The war raged and India was fighting on all fronts. Lal Bahadur Shastri, the then Prime Minister coined the term "Jai Jawan Jai Kisan" and galvanized the nation into patriotic fervour. Madan mobilized the resources to help the soldiers on the frontline. There were rumours afloat about

Pakistani infiltrators reaching big cities of India including Delhi and poisoning the water sources. Madan organized local defence schemes in his locality to guard all vulnerable points, though fortunately nothing happened and all ended well with India's victory over Pakistan in the war.

As planned Madan purchased a very big bungalow for himself in Rajouri Garden. He was now among the list of leading business men of Delhi. He had spread his business up to Calcutta, which was being looked after by one of his trusted executives. Madan's acquaintance had also spread in Calcutta, since he had to very often visit there. Madan displayed the photographs of Late Lala Ram Lal, his grand father and of Late lala Hari Ram his father, in the gallery of the new house which he just purchased in Rajouri garden. He had managed to carry these pictures with him to be passed on to posterity. Now that Raj was also growing and he and Reena had only known about late parents and family of Madan; that too during the course of normal conversation, they were very curious to learn about their ancestral history. It was Sunday and Raj requested his father Madan to tell them something about their family history.

Raj was too delighted to see the keen-ness on the part of Raj about the subject and he narrated the salient issues of interest to them. "When I think of my past, I remember my childhood and one time happy family. These pictures as you know are of my late grandfather and my late father. I did not see my grand father but I was told he died very young due to heart failure. My father was probably in his teens then. Though financially we were not very rich but my grand father was a known person since he took active part in politics. My father was already married at the time of my grand father's death and my mother took care of my grand mother, who also left at the age of around 50 years.

My grandma did not allow my father to indulge in any kind of politics which she always abhorred. My father Lala Hari Ram was a thorough gentle man and very honest. People in the village respected him for that. We did not have much but whatever we had we were contented with. The only source of income was a small grocery shop in the village, which father managed and managed it too well. He was emotionally attached to it. We just had one or two pairs of clothes. It was on the occasion of major festivals ie. Diwali or Holi that we took out our new clothes from the steel box of my mother. Incase some of us did not find one, he or she would keep crying till one is brought from the market. My mother who also preserved her silk sari of marriage, would take it out from the box and wear it to join the other ladies going for pooja. We were all very happy particularly on Diwali that each one of us got sweets to our full requirement. Any carry forward of sweets by anyone, used to be point of quarrel amongst us. Though of course, my mother always favoured me to be the son and the youngest of all. Sometimes my father could not afford to buy us new books, and instead he would get us second hand from the bazaar. Even I recall, I was without lantern for my final metric examination and had shared with my friend Omi. But God was kind and we were a very happy family, till final stroke of misfortunes which brought unbearable calamity and engulfed the entire happiness. The story beyond that I have already told you a number of time and I do not wish to repeat it since it is very painful for me," Said Madan with his eyes red, filled with tears.

Once there was a small delegation comprising of mainly village panchayat of village Rajgarh, came to Madan with a proposal to make some more building in the existing school which was up to Middle standard.

"Sahib, there are about seven-eight people, waiting at the gate to meet you. They all are from your village Rajgarh," Told the gatekeeper to Madan who was inside the bungalow.

Hearing this Madan got so excited that without even bothering for what dress he was wearing, he ran to the gate to meet the gram panchayat of his village, the memories of which were still very fresh in his mind and he used to cherish them.

"Namaste, Uncle Rampat and to others. Come, it is your bungalow, why have you all stopped here on the gate," Very respectfully said Madan.

Rampat in addition to being the Sarpanch was the man of high social standing in the village. Madan took them to his big drawing room, made them sit and personally got involved in looking after them. How greatness and humility could co-exist could be seen in Madan. Madan charmed his guests with eloquence and fine intensity of his manners.

"Why are you so excited? Let servants do their jobs in looking after the guests. Guests have not come to our house for the first time," Said Reena to Madan.

"Oh, Reena you can not appreciate my emotions and feelings for these men and for my village, even a little message from that village excites me, now there is full panchayat of that village in my house. I owe everything to my birth place, Rajgarh; Is it not a cause of happiness and excitement?", Said Madan.

By now Reena had sensed the high emotions and a typical happiness on the face of Madan. She too started preparing tea and eatables herself in the kitchen. Madan and Reena personally served and looked after these people from their villave. Even the people of gram panchayat were overwhelmed with the courtesis and treatment they received in a palatial house from such a rich person, much against their expectations.

"Yes, Uncle Rampat (who was the Sarpanch of the Gram panchayat), what use could I be to the village," Very humbly asked Madan.

"Son, the school that you also studied in, now needs to be upgraded to 10th class. Government wants the village to make building for extra classes, only then it can be upgraded. You know the village is very poor and panchayat also has not development funds to meet this big requirement," Said Rampat.

"Uncle please do not hesitate, tell me how much would this cost, I shall bear the entire cost," Said Madan.

"There is requirement of three additional class rooms and one big hall, total of four. This as per our estimate, would cost approximately Rupees twenty thousands," Said Kanhiya Lal another member of the panchayat.

Madan made out a cheque of Rs 20,000/- in the name of gram panchayat for the construction of school and handed over to Rampat the Sarpanch. Madan was very happy after making this donation, for the noblest cause in his thinking. Habit of helping others was ingrained in him.

The school building was made as per plan and it was upgraded to class 10th also by the government. The building had a plate on it which read, "Made in the Sweetest memory of Lala Hari Ram, with the kind and generous donation from his son Lala Madan Lal."

Life was happily passing for Madan. He was now about 45 years of age. His son Raj was also growing well. He was doing his schooling. Reena spent most of her time in looking after the house though she was regular in her daily pooja (worship). Madan was quite contented in life. He had started donating a part of his income for religious work and for the help of poor people. He was very kind hearted and generous.

One day a case was reported to him of one of his factory manager who had made about rupees fifty thousands by fraud in the factory. The matter was as usual reported to the police who started their normal investigations; during which the accused confessed and was to be jailed. However manager's wife who had two marriageable daughters, went to Madan's house to beg for mercy. The gate keeper who was also aware of the misdeeds of her husband would not let her in. Good luck for the lady, it was late in the evening and Madan came out of the house to the lawn. Madan noticed the lady with her daughters standing at the gate and weeping.

"Who are they," Asked Madan walking up to the gate, from the gate keeper.

"She is that Manager's wife and wants to meet you," Replied the gate keeper.

"Yes, lady what can I do for you," Asked Madan from the lady.

"You are our God, you can save our lives including the lives of these two girls," Told manager's wife crying.

"Yes, I know the case, your husband whom I trusted so much has betrayed my faith. If he needed money he should have asked for help from the company," Said Madan.

"Poverty is a curse on a human being. We have these two marriageable daughters and the people are asking for dowry which my husband with just meager pay alone can not cater for, he is an honest person, has been your employee for over 10 years, but circumstances have driven him to this miserable state where he had to steal and land up now in jail. You can only save this family from getting totally ruined," Pleaded manager's wife crying and touching Madan's feet.

"Do not touch my feet, I am not a God. I am also a human being, probably with better control over myself than your husband. Such difficult occasions come in everyone's life in some shape, but only weaker ones succumb to these pressures and land up in a shameful situation like your husband," Said Madan.

"I shall excuse him for once since I do not want to be cause of a ruin of one well settled family. But tell your husband to keep control over his senses," Further added Madan.

Madan having said that went back to his house with some sense of satisfaction that he had been of some use to the humanity. He asked his Personal manager to withdraw the case against the manager and was asked to resume his service.

Time was passing well. God was kind to both the families ie Madan's and Harlal's, his father in law. Years passed. Harlal and Kunti grew old. Their both sons also got married in good families one from Delhi itself and another one from Jaipur in Rajasthan. Harlal had generally retired and his business was now being looked after by his both the sons.

Madan's business was also flourishing. His son Raj was in B Commerce final year in Delhi University. His bent of mind was also more towards business. He used to give lot of suggestions to Madan about business and accountancy. Madan was happy seeing the interest of his only son in his business and always felt satisfied that his business will pass on to Competent hands. Reena devoted most of her time reading religious books and in her pooja, of course in addition to looking after the house hold which though was mostly being managed by the servants.

Raj was very brilliant in studies and strictly followed the value system of the life same way as father Madan. It was a co education college of Delhi where Raj was studying. But this aspect did not affect him since he had the least interest in befriending a girl. He had a close friend Ravi in the same class, who was from Allahabad and stayed in a room in the college hostel. Ravi was also topper in his studies that is how they became close friends. Though Ravi was not from an affluent family but was aspiring to join the elite administrative services after his graduation. Raj used to spend one to two hours in Ravi's room soon after the college hours for studying and sharing notes. There appeared to be a very close, happy competetion between the two, as to who would top the merit in B com, that year.

After the summer vacations when Ravi was returning from Allahabad to Delhi, he got into a compartment in which a girl named Sheema, a student of arts in his college was also travelling from Bombay; coming back to Delhi, her home city, after the summer break. They became known to each other and over a period of time, their relations developed into a close friendship. Ravi and Sheema would often meet in the college cafe and go for cinema on holidays. Raj was not aware of this development. Ravi knew Raj's principles in life and for the fear of losing a good friend he kept it to himself. As time passed, Raj noticed a gradual change in the behaviour and conduct of Ravi. He used to remain lost in the class and often asked for financial help from Raj which he never did earlier. Raj could notice something wrong and one day probed into his privacy.

"Hope all is well at home," Asked Raj from Ravi.

"Yes, all is perfectly well. I just spoke to my mother on the telephone," Replied Ravi.

Raj did not feel like probing it any further at that juncture, but he was sure that all was not well with Ravi. As a friend Raj was also feeling concerned and wanted to be of some help to Ravi. Raj planned to visit Ravi on coming Sunday to try once more, if Ravi could share his problems with him. As planned he went to Ravi's room at around 11 AM in the hostel and found it locked. Since Raj had the duplicate key of the room from the beginning for studies, he opened the room and wanted to go through some of the notes of Ravi as a routine. Since it was an impromptu visit, Ravi left his room untidy and seemed to leave in a hurry. Raj picked up that day's newspaper from Ravi's bed just to glance through, he noticed a personal diary that Ravi used to write daily. Out of curiosity he read through a few pages and was amazed to find his infatuation for Sheema. It further read "God has been kind to me that I found such a beautiful girl who would make an excellent life partner." Raj cursed him self for his ignorance and simplicity that he was incapable of knowing even such an important event in his close friend's life for the past six months or so. Of course now he was able to find the reasons for difference in Ravi's behaviour and attitude towards his studies which had become somewhat casual.

Next day, Raj did not even mention to Ravi about visiting his room on Sunday. He wanted to speak to Ravi at length since it was a private and sensitive matter. As usual he accompanied Ravi soon after the college to his room in the garb of studying.

"Who is Sheema and how have you got to know her," Asked Raj from Ravi when they were just about to start their academic discussions.

Ravi was shocked that Raj was aware of his friendship with Sheema which he had been trying hard all these days to conceal it from him. Now that there was no other way out, Ravi thought it prudent to share it with Raj in confidence.

Ravi told the entire episode and also divulged his intention of ultimately marrying Sheema. Raj advised him to first finish his studies and get settled before adding anything to his financial liabilities. Raj even told Ravi to be sure of the girl's credentials which at time turn out to be otherwise, particularly for girls with cosmopolitan background. Though Ravi appeared to be too sure of all the details; since that was his first love and an encounter with a girl and he was emotionally involved. Ravi spoke of all the praises for Sheema and any further advice from Raj appeared indigestible for him, which Raj also could read.

In addition to studies in the college, Ravi's affair with Sheema went on. Raj had reduced his visits to his room to the bearest minimum since he found Ravi mostly pre occupied and obsessed with meeting Sheema as much as he could. Raj who hardly had any interest in such affairs started feeling about Ravi to be lucky to find a suitable girl for him.

It was a New year's eve and Ravi wanted Sheema to accompany him to a club for celebrations which she declined on the pretext of being very un well. He then rang up Raj for the company which he agreed, more so because Ravi's talks abouts his love affairs had started interesting him.

They went to a club in Delhi around 11 PM. They found the crowd high with liquor and most of them were dancing on the floor. Raj and Ravi sat in the corner since chairs in the center were already occupied. The lights inside the hall were slightly dim by design. As they both were watching the crowd, Ravi's eyes caught on a dancing couple who were closely hugging each other, he found the lady to be Sheema, his love and would be life partner. He got a jolt. He walked up to that couple even without telling Raj and tapped Sheema's shoulders. Sheema looked at Ravi but pretended not to recognize him. When Ravi tried to pull her to side, she gave him a slap. In the meantime Raj also reached the scene and did not allow the situation to take ugly turn. They immediately returned to Ravi's hostel who was now crest fallen. Raj tried to pacify him that there was no dearth of good girls. Raj only left his room late in the night when he was convinced that Ravi would go to sleep. Next day when Raj came to college he found lot of gathering in the hostel near Ravi's room. He immediately rushed and found that Ravi had jumped from his third floor room and died. This badly shook Raj's faith and love for the woman. This tragedy left lasting impression on Raj.

One day there was a telephone call from Harlal to Madan informing him about some relations marriage outside Delhi.

"Madan have you got an invitation for marriage of Kunti's cousin at Mount Abu, in Rajasthan next month" Asked Harlal.

"Yes, we got it day before," Confirmed Madan.

"How do you plan going? Why can't we go together since we are now old and if you and Reena are with us, it will be nice," Asked Harlal from Madan.

"I was also thinking the same way. Infact Reena was suggesting this, that you are not too well and we all should go together," Replied Madan.

The programme was fixed and they all planned to go to Mount Abu together to attend the marriage. Though they took two cars but Harlal, Kunti, Madan and Reena were travelling in one car and second car was a follow up, occupied by the driver and one servant.

It was an excellent gathering at Mount Abu. Reena's Uncle though belonged to Ajmer had shifted his business to Mount Abu long back. There were a few guests from Calcutta and Assam also who had come to attend the marriage.

"Madan, come I shall introduce you to Lala Chet Ram who is a very big business man of Calcutta and owns two cotton mills and other small outfits; we are good friends and old classmates," Introduced Harlal.

"Chet Ram, he is my son in law, Madan Lal a very big industrialist in Delhi and has a factory in Calcutta also," Further introduced Harlal.

Both Madan and Chet Ram exchanged pleasantries and then all three of them settled down on chairs on the lawn of the hotel where the marriage was being solemnized. Infact Harlal and Lala Chet Ram were talking for a long time standing separately on one side before Madan was called and introduced.

"Madan, Lala Chet Ram has one daughter who has finished her BA and one son who is in BA final; both are studying in Calcutta only. The girl has lot of hobbies and accomplished in tailoring, cooking and fabric designing etc. She is charming conversationist and won prize for best oration at her college," Said Harlal.

"That is wonderful to have such talented children," Replied Madan.

"He is keen in our Raj for his daughter, I have checked they are of the same age group, the girl is about six months younger," Informed Harlal.

"That is OK, babuji, you may talk to Reena also about it, we can discuss it later in Delhi, since we have sometime till Raj completes his B Com this year," Said Madan.

Marriage went on well. All the guests were leaving. Madan and Harlal also planned to leave for Delhi. It was about 8 AM they left Mount Abu in their car in the similar manner as they came. Madan, Reena, Harlal and Kunti were in one car, followed by the second car with a driver and a servant. All were very happy with the arrangement made in the marriage at Mount Abu and were talking about it.

"Yes, Reena, I wanted to tell you about Lala Chet Ram, who was there in the marriage from Calcutta, a very rich business man, he was proposing his daughter for our Raj," Told Harlal.

"Yes, daddy, I noticed three of you discussing something seriously last evening sitting outside in the lawn of the hotel," Said Reena.

"If you know them and if the girl is good it should be alright," Further said Reena.

Kunti—We will make better arrangement than this marriage in our Raj's marriage so that the people find a change.

Harlal—Of course, we will do our best in Raj's marriage.

The visit to the hill station was a great triumph enormously enjoyed by all, a distant change from living in over crowded Delhi.

The car was going down slope since Mount Abu is a hill station. There are a number of sharp turns on the road which need a careful driving from a new driver on this road. As ill luck would have it, on one of the turns while avoiding collision with a truck coming up from opposite direction, the driver of the car-swerved dangerously and lost control, bashed into the parapet and went straight down the hill. The car having rolled down went about hundred meters in a nalah (a water stream) and caught fire. The people seeing the accident rushed to the car to help the passengers. Unfortunately by the time they could be rescued, Harlal, Kunti and Reena who were on the back seat of the car had already died. Madan and the driver who were on the front, got thrown out, though badly bruised, but survived.

It was once again a big shock in the life for Madan when he was left alone in this world. Similar conditions prevailed when his father had died of heart attack, after the fire incident in the village when he was just 18 years of age. Though now about fifty plus, but he lost his loving wife and parents like in laws who helped him settle so well in life. It was again a near total black out for Madan who so heavily depended on these people for emotional and moral support.

Man proposes but God disposes, proved absolutely correct here. They were planning for the marriage of Raj while travelling in the car, but it was not to be, and the destiny struck them within no time and so hard. After this tragedy Madan had miserable time, had no peace of mind, no sleep and often used to be absent minded and his replies were mechanical and incoherent.

Death of Reena had very adverse effect on Madan. He lost iterest in his business and changed over to devoting time in reading religious books and scriptures. Raj who had finished his B Com education, started looking after his business on behalf of his father. Two years had past, life seemed to be coming to normal. A changed routine after the death of Reena had come into being for Madan, who had left most of the business to Raj who was now quite grown up and matured at the age of about 23 years. The absence of a female member in such a big house was conspicuous. Time was ripe that a suitable girl was found for Raj. Madan was rich and benevolent owner of one of the largest estates in Delhi and his oddly assorted house. His wealth and reputation attracted number of fortune hunting people for Raj's marriage. Though Raj was not too keen for marriage after the death of his friend Ravi and treated it as a family obligation.

One day there was a call from one of the acquaintances of Madan from Calcutta.

"Madan I am Rajbir speaking from Calcutta," Said the voice from the other end.

"Oh, Rajbir how are you? It is long time we spoke. What a pleasure to hear you today," Spoke Madan.

"I know the tragedy you have faced. Bhabi ji has gone leaving you all alone at this old age when you needed her the most," Said Rajbir.

"It is God's wish, no one can do anything about it," Replied Madan.

"I wanted to speak to you about Raj's marriage, now that he is grown up and settled and also there is an urgent requirement of a female member in your house," Spoke Rajbir.

"Yes, you are right Rajbir. I am also looking for some suitable match for the young boy," Said Madan.

"You know Lala Chet Ram of Calcutta who met you in that marriage at Mount Abu about three years ago, he has been wanting a reply from you. He did not raise the matter earlier because of that tragedy," Said Rajbir on telephone.

"Please ask Lala Chet Ram to come over to Delhi. He can see the boy and our house hold, the environment in our house where his daughter has to settle down for her life," Spoke Madan.

"OK, he shall get in touch with you and fix a date to visit you in Delhi," Said Rajbir closing the conversation.

After a week, Lala Chet Ram came to Delhi to meet Madan. He was very happy to see the business and atmosphere of Madan's house. Raj was also found most suitable match for his daughter Priya. He had brought a photo of his daughter, which was approved by Madan also. The marriage was fixed for the coming month and Chet Ram happily returned to Calcutta.

Priya was beautiful, tall, fair and possessed excellent features. She was young and charming with modern outlook which could draw any young man to her. Though Lala Chet Ram fixed the marriage of his daughter Priya with Raj, the son of Madan but he was not aware that Priya was in love with Mr Prem, one of his managers who often visited Chet Ram's house in connection with official work and the two fell in love with each other. Prem was an ambitious young man who wanted to acquire wealth by any means. His showing love for Priya was more for money than sincere love, which she was not able to decipher. No one in the family had any knowledge of this relationship developing, except

Chet Ram's old widowed sister Rajni, who did sense the brewing a little.

Chet Ram returned from Delhi in the afternoon and told the family about the engagement of Priya and Raj. Mohan, son of Chet Ram complimented his sister Priya which was answered by her with downcast looks and monosyllables which was taken as a sign of modern assent; particularly in the presence of Chet Ram. Chet Ram also was happy seeing change in Priya's attitude, who earlier opposed marrying Raj on flimsy grounds. Perceiving her father in a fit of affection, Priya thought she would never have a better opportunity of disclosing her feeling than that time. She laid hold of his hand and falling on her knees she begged him not to make her the most miserable creature on earth by forcing her to marry a man who she did not know. She said, "Not only your poor Priya's happiness but her very life, her being, depends upon your granting her request. I can not live with Raj. To force me into this marriage would be killing me". But Chet Ram concluded in these words, "I am resolved upon the match and unless you consent to it I will not give you a grout, not a single farthing, I would rather see you die in this room. This is my fixed resolution and so I leave you to consider on it."

When Chet Ram came out of the room of Priya he found Prem in the hall. Prem seeing Chet Ram wild, pale and almost breathless, inquired the reason of his melancholy. Upon which Chet Ram acquainted him with the whole matter. Prem was at first almost struck dead with this revelation. Recovering his spirit, he desired to meet Priya and try to persuade her to agree to her father's inclinations. Little knowing that Prem himself loved Priya, Chet Ram asked him to go and do whatever he could to convince her to accept her marriage proposal.

Coming to Priya's room he found her just risen from the ground where her father had left her, with tears trickling from her eyes. He ran to her and told her about his love for her. Both stood for a time hand in hand, silent and trembling at the thought of their separation; particularly for Prem who could see his plans failing. Prem asked Priya to promise that she would never give herself to Raj of Delhi, which Priya assured him; being in sincere love with him.

Soon after Prem left, his sister Rajni came there. When Chet Ram told her that Priya was refusing to marry Raj, she informed him that his daughter was in love with Prem. Chet Ram stood for a moment like a person struck with thunder and then rushed into the room of Priya roaring forth threats of revenge at every step. Priya was so frightened to hear the thunderous voice of her father that she fainted. She was soon restored to her consciousncss with the help of water by Rajni.

No sooner was Chet Ram cured of his immediate fears for his daughter, than he relapsed into his frenzy which produced an immediate battle with Prem. Having reached the office Chet Ram called Prem to his chamber and gave him mouthful for his betrayal of faith and playing with the honour of his family. Having been caught for his ill designs Prem was shivering and was unable to utter a single word in support of his actions. Chet Ram dismissed Prem from the job and commanded him to leave the complex immediately. Prem having been caught, found this the best way to get away, lest should he be handed over to the Police. He accordingly disappeared once for all without even talking to Priya; with whom he was never in true love. Of course Priya could never know about it. She did not believe the version of her parents when she was informed about Prem's game plan.

Mrs Chet Ram summoned Priya to her room and told her that her father had resolved to marry her immediately with Raj in Delhi. But Priya cried out, "Indeed this is the only instance in which I must disobey you all; for this is a match which requires very little consideration in me to refuse." Mrs Chet Ram insisted that she ought to have a greater regard for the honour of the family than for her own person. Priya replied, "I shall never do anything to dishonour my family, but I should not marry Raj, whom I do not even know." Chet Ram who had been in the hearing, was now exhausted of all his patience and entered the room in a violent passion and began to unfold the ill designs of Prem because of whom she was bent upon rejecting the suitable match with Raj. Chet Ram was so enraged that he declared to leave the house if Priya did not agree to marry Raj. Since Priya got totally isolated she very hesitatingly agreed to marry Raj. The marriage of Priya and Raj was solemnized as per original programme and new bride Priya moved to Delhi with Raj; though not very happy with the entire proceedings since she still had not forgotten Prem and that Raj was slightly inferior to her in appearance and physical profile.

Priya was a modern girl from Calcutta with a modern outlook. She was brought up in a very rich culture and educated in convent schools. There appeared slight mismatch in the culture of two families ie Lala Chet Ram and Madan. Raj had a mix bringing up ie, education in convent schools but religious atmosphere at home. He was trying to keep up with the changed style of Priya in the house. Raj was too impressed with her beauty and modern culture that he could not say anything to Priya. Though Madan was not happy with Priya's conduct and Raj's abetment.

Love was not a passion with Raj. He preferred to remain contained and reserved. His business first and love after-wards was, what he thought. His main concern was to see if she could fit into their social template.

Priya brought new music system and new records of modern songs, which replaced the old bhajan (religious songs) and the general environment of the house. At times Priya called her girl friends who were also married in Delhi for meals where there used to be dance and music, much to the dislike of Madan. She belonged to an age of transition where belief in absolute values were eroding and old religious belief were becoming invalid. She was frank, talked openly about sex matters and other such subjects without timidity or mock modesty.

Madan who was in his early sixties, got isolated in such an atmosphere and he preferred to stay in his room which was in one corner of the house. Though he did not like all the happenings in his house, particularly the behavior and conduct of Priya with everyone. Though she was respectful to him. His belief that all the ladies are by nature good, pious, religious and kind hearted was gradually fading away. Madan patiently tolerated Priya's grossness and profanity for the sake of peace in the house which once was a godly abode. The spirit of emancipation was nowhere seen to better advantage in the freedom that Priya gradually acquired in that house. Other wise the place of woman at that time was within the four walls of the house; any contact with the outside world was supposed to corrupt and spoil them. Their sole business was to look after the comforts of their manfolk.

Madan was once again all alone in that big empire he had created from the scratch. Madan had set his routine of morning and evening walks, reading religious books and pooja both the times. He had become very tolerant in the interest of peace in the house and was keen to see his son settle down with that modern girl, even at the cost of his seclusion.

Two years passed since the marriage of his son Raj. Business was flourishing well. Madan was now about 65 years of age. He was very particular about his routine. He had made a few friends in the neighborhood of similar age groups who used to go for walk with Madan and at times exchanged views sitting in the public park.

One day after the morning walk Madan returned home, accompanied by a friend of same age. It was about 10 AM. He made his friend sit in the drawing room, where he had probably entered after few months that too with a friend.

"Priya, please arrange two cups of tea for us," Said Madan sitting in the drawing room with his friend.

"It is no time for tea, the kitchen has already been done up by the servant," Very offensively replied Priya.

Having said that Priya went to her bathroom to take bath. Madan who was such a rich person and a known industrialist, felt very ashamed in front of his friend that in his own house, he could not even get two cups of tea, when needed. Not showing his anger Madan got up, asking the friend to keep sitting and went to kitchen to make tea himself.

The lady, who was still in her room, heard the sound of utensils from the kitchen, came back, rebuked Madan for his impatience and put off the gas. Sensing some trouble Madan's friend had already left. Madan also went to his room. He was feeling totally ransacked and broken in his own house. He even cried in his room, remembering Reena. Madan never completely got over the shock of her tragic death. Reena was a highly devoted wife. He felt totally helpless person feeling as if hell had fallen on him. He was feeling utterly guilty and shameful as what face would this known industrialist will show to his friends next day for the morning walk. He was totally restless and remained awake the whole night. Madan was again in similar situation as was, when he was leaving his village for Delhi after the death of his father. A near total break down of nervous system. Madan felt dubious and discontented and wondered whether he was really and truly successful as a human being.

Next day passed, Madan did not go out of the house, nor did he show any annoyance to his own son or Priya, but kept it burning inside himself. As per earlier plan Priya and Raj were leaving that night for Calcutta for a few days in connection with business. Though the entire business still continued to be in the name of Madan as 'Madan Enterprises'. Madan was a luminary in industrial circle of Delhi.

Following day Madan called his lawyer and asked him to prepare sale deeds of entire 'Madan Enterprises' and the house in which they were living. Madan who had still not overcome the shock and was feeling very deeply hurt, sold everything in Delhi, except his old two roomed small house in Tri Nagar and a small factory of Calcutta; leaving only that much for his son to subsist on.

Madan having sold everything in Delhi, left the keys of Tri Nagar house with same neighbour who had come with Madan for tea after morning walk and knew the entire episode. He left Delhi for his birth place Rajgarh, once for all.

After a few days, Raj returned to Delhi with his wife Priya. He came straight to their house in Rajouri Garden from the airport. He was already little suspicious since he did not find any car at the airport to bring them home, since their entire programme including date and time of return flight was known to the management.

Having reached his house in a taxi, they found their house locked from outside, no gatekeeper or any known face was around. Raj started shouting for the servant who was working with the family for a number of years. Hearing Raj yelling, the old man from the neighbouring house came out.

"Why are you shouting, disturbing the entire locality." Asked the old man.

"Uncle, where all these people have disappeared including my father," Said Raj in a commanding tone.

"Son, here there is nothing which belongs to you. Your father has sold the entire 'Madan Enterprises' including this house and has gone back to Rajgarh, his village," Told the old man.

"Was he mad? How could he do that without our knowledge," Angrily asked Priya, duly shocked.

It looked so silly and incredible on part of this lady, speaking like this about such a reputed and a highly respected person, all present there thought.

"No, he was mad all along, but fortunately you awakened him by insulting him in my presence that day when he asked you for tea and you declined and rebuked that saintly person," Retorted the old man clicking his tongue in disgust at Priya.

Listening the conversation lot of people from the locality had gathered, most of them knew the entire episode. The old man told the complete incident to Raj and the conditions under which Madan had to take that decision.

Raj also broke down and sat on a stool of the neighbouring tea shop like a petrified sentry. The old man took out the keys of Tri Nagar house and gave it to Raj.

"He was a very loving father, the owner of one fourth of Delhi's industries, but you and your wife reduced him to a non- entity," Very angrily spoke the old man.

"Madan was still a very considerate father and has left that two roomed house in Tri Nagar and factory of Calcutta for you, otherwise he would have reduced you to begging, seeing your and your wife's conduct and behaviour with him and enjoying his earnings," Said another old person from the gathering.

Seeing the condition of her husband. Raj, his wife Priya grew very solicitous, obviously she suffered from guilt of insulting Madan (his father) and tried to compensate for her wifely devotion. Raj was not in his usual self and was losing a great deal of his mental relaxation. He was thinking what to do next since he had several problems to contend with. He became nervous and sensitive and full of anxiety in various ways.

The lady Priya was still in anger and talking loosely. The crowd started shouting shame, shame for her. Seeing the situation, Raj got into the same taxi and drove off towards Tri Nagar.

V

Madan reached his village Rajgarh in his chauffeur driven car and with two more servants who used to work for Madan in Delhi also. It was in the afternoon that Madan reached the village. The villagers were generally surprised with the sudden arrival of Madan after a long time. Madan got his house opened and asked the servants to clean it up. There was old furniture, a few cots were lying in the house, of Hari Ram's time (vintage). Madan got things organized and sat in the same room in which he slept on the night prior to his leaving the village for Delhi when he was just about 18 years of age. Now Madan was about 67 years old and depended on others for care and help; which of course was available in abundance due to his position and status in the society. What was now missing was his family, despite his being very rich. He was probably getting realization about the futility of accumulation of unwanted wealth and artificiality and selfishness of close blood relations; that only made him take such a strong step to dispose off everything and return to his village Rajgarh.

"Namaste Lala ji," Said Rampat the sarpanch of the village to Madan.

"Come Rampat Uncle, in fact I was thinking of you only," Replied Madan.

"What a pleasant surprise, seeing you here, uninformed," Said Rampat.

"Yes, Rampat Uncle, life in Delhi was becoming too boring without any work at this age and there was no worth while company. I then decided to return to our village and devote rest of my life in some social work," Said Madan.

"It is excellent and good luck for this backward village which needs you the most." Very happily replied Rampat.

It is already late in the evening I think you come over tomorrow around 9 AM, we shall go around the village to see what use I could be to the people here," Said Madan to Rampat.

The servants of Madan with the help of villagers had cleaned the house and, the cook made evening meal in the house itself since they had come fully prepared and equipped from Delhi.

Madan had a mixed feeling of having returned to the village. He did not have sound sleep since he was not used to sleeping without air-conditioners. Though he got up quite fresh and energetic with some noble objectives and aims in his mind for the good of the people of village and area around. Money was no problem with Madan, he had only to identify the suitable community projects and a dedicated and honest team of people from the village to supervise the execution of the works.

Next few days, Madan spent time going around the village and discussing the social work he intended to undertake. First of all the construction of village temple and the school play field with an auditorium was done. Madan also got the road made up-to the village, which was around one kilometer short. He had also informed the sarpanches of other adjoining villages through Rampat that when ever any girl belonging to poor parents gets married he should be informed so that he could help monetarily as per their needs. The deserving students of the area were given stipend by him for further education.

Within one year Madan became a known person of repute in the area around Sikar that people brought to him disputes of ancestral problems. He had set apart a few hours in the afternoon for these activities. He could hardly afford a private life now. There came a stage when he had to be up early morning and rush through all his personal routine before his visitors arrived. It was a strain upon him and he yearned for quiet and peaceful life. He was also not very happy with the pace of work he was getting executed in the entire area around Rajgarh.

Though fame of his generosity and social work spread up to Sikar city. One day delegation from Sikar also approached him for some help for the orphanage and gowshala (cow raring place). They even requested Madan to organize drinking water on the railway station when ever the trains passed through Sikar railway station.

Madan conceded to all these demands and executed these very happily. In addition to the above, Madan even started giving free cooked food to the passengers on the railway platform during lunch time. People of the entire area treated Madan as a God sent person for their up-liftment. By now Madan was highly respected in all the segment of society including the district administration of Sikar. The circle of his admirers had vastly increased. His effusion of love for people and his good nature impelled Madan to promote good relations among all and this exalted him to a position of a devta (God man) in the area.

About two years had past. Madan had spent most of his money on the good of the humanity. But he had started getting some kind of a feeling that his job there was generally over and that he should move somewhere closer to God who had been so kind to Madan. Even some of the activities of the people involved in execution of work, put him off, for some of them were not honest even in the work meant for religious purposes and God. He got totally disillusioned and wanted to renounce the world to find inner harmony and lasting peace.

Since Madan had created a big infrastructure in the area, he wanted it to continue even when he left, he made a trust with a few known people as trustees. Madan made the trust a viable and self sustaining unit to function for times to come. Their main function included maintenance of buildings, help to needy, stipend to deserving students and continuance of meal service at the railway station at Sikar. Madan had gifted enough of money to the trust for it to run smoothly for ever, since his projects also included construction of commercial shops along side Dharamshala etc which were a big source of income for the trust.

Madan was getting restless, his soul was pressing him hard to move out for a higher goal somewhere close to God to lead a life of simplicity, sincerity and harmony. There was a religious functions in the temple one day in the evening. He asked all of his helpers also to go to mela, which was to continue till mid night. He after sun set left his village without telling anyone in his car up to railway station and boarded a train and left Sikar for ever.

When the helpers returned from the mela in the night, they did not find Madan in the room, nor was his car there. They waited till morning and then informed the sarpanch, Rampat. The entire village set out looking for Madan. Somebody reached the railway station also at Sikar and found Madan's car parked there. Rampat and other trustees all reached the railway station when they opened the car, found a hand written note by Madan kept on the seat which read, "Do not look for me, you will waste your time. I have finished my job here. Now God wants me to do something better and I am going there; no one can reach me. We are living in a troubled world which is in turmoil. Negativity pervades it and many of us have weary souls which need spiritual help."

The people of entire area were very sad as if hell had fallen on them. They considered it their misfortune. They were totally direction-less and felt as if God had withdrawn all his blessings once showered upon them. But as the time past people started getting to normal. This is the law of nature, time is the best healer. The trustees took on the responsibility as a challenge to fullfill Madan's wishes. They were not even sure whether Madan was still alive. As a mark of respect to commemorate his services to the society, Madan's statues were installed at a number of public places. Madan left behind his lasting fragrance of love and compassion.

The driver of the car returned to Delhi after Madan left Rajgarh. He informed Raj about the entire activities that took place in Rajgarh and retired from the service since he had been very sincere and loyal to Madan for over 25 years. The driver was also feeling very sad about the sudden disappearance of Madan from Rajgarh; since he was very close and confident of Madan. He was feeling guilty as to what went wrong that Lala Madan lal did not even inform him about his plans, which had never happened in the past.

"Why are you looking slightly unhappy," Asked Priya from Raj when he returned home that evening.

"No, it is not much, I am not feeling too well today," replied Raj.

"Should I get you some medicine," Again asked Priya.

"No, this pain will not go with the medicine, it will take little time and will disappear itself," Said Raj.

"What is it about? Why can't you share it with me at least," insisted Priya.

Raj could not hold any longer and told the entire story to Priya including his father Madan disappearing all of a sudden without telling anyone in the village or to other trustees.

"Good thing, he should have in fact disappeared earlier, lot of People would have benefited," Very curtly said Priya.

"No, darling he was my father after all, I shall have to go looking for him," Replied Raj.

"Don't be silly, your father never treated you as a son and left you all alone, totally helpless and nearly penniless," Said Priya in anger, who had yet not been chastened by the drubbings.

"Yes darling, but what should I do now?" Asked Raj.

"Let us go to club, we will have our dinner there and forget about that old man, in anycase, this was the age for him to go." Said Priya.

Raj found Priya incorrigible and hesitatingly got ready and they both went to the club. Night passed. Next day morning Raj was getting ready to go to his office in Tri Nagar and Priya was still asleep. Raj woke her up before moving to dinning table for breakfast. Priya also joined him on the table with a cup of tea in her hand, still yawning.

"Raj, I got an idea, I shall tell you only if you, firmly act upon it," Said Priya.

"Yes Priya, please tell me what is it? I shall certainly act if it suits our interest," Said Raj.

Your father has invested the entire money in various projects in your village. There is a trust which is managing this entire thing and enjoying its income too. Why can't you go there to Rajgarh and claim all this and take charge on behalf of your father. In any case you are his real heir," Advised Priya.

Raj—No I can not go there. People will laugh at me since I did not visit my father even once after he returned to Rajgarh.

Priya—Why did you have to visit him, the way he left You. He did not deserve a bit of it. Do not let these silly points bother you.

Raj—OK, I shall go tomorrow. Will you also like to come with me?

Priya—No, I do not want to go to that remote place again. I had got bored when I was taken there with you for some local devta pooja, soon after the marriage. You go alone. Do not worry for anything. Be firm and assertive.

Raj as planned left for Rajgarh the next day. He did not go to the village and instead stayed at Sikar city in a hotel. Next day, he went to the Trust office which was located in Sikar it-self. He met one of the trustees who happened to be there in the office at that time. Raj told them everything that he wanted to take charge of the entire trust which belonged to his father Madan.

The trustee sent for Rampat the sarpanch who was the head of the trust and informed all others too. Rampat along with other people of the village and adjoining area went to the trust office next day to meet Raj the son of Madan. All concerned people reached there as was told.

"Yes Raj, what do you want" Asked Rampat.

"I want the entire property of my father since I am the real heir," Replied Raj.

"Lala Madan Lal had no son as per his will, where have you come from all of a sudden, that too after he has gone," Jokingly said another member of the trust.

"Where were you when your wife insulted him and you did not even bother to come and meet him even once in Rajgarh." Said yet another person present there, angrily.

"As per our knowledge and official record and his will, Lala Madan lal had no son, because if he had a son, he would have taken care of Madan in his old age," Said Rampat.

Raj got angry and said "I shall take you all to the court, you do not otherwise understand normal language." He stoutly protested but no one agreed with Raj.

The entire gathering got shocked and terribly annoyed on the way this young man Raj behaved and threatened.

"You better disappear from here fast before any unpleasant thing happens," All of them said.

Raj could sense trouble and realized that he was on wrong footings. He left empty handed not to return to Rajgarh again, Of course cursing Priya all along his journey back to Delhi for her wrong advice.

VI

Lala Madan Lal having reached Sikar Railway station, left his car there itself and caught a train at mid time, going to Delhi. Though it was the month of April, when there were lot of people roaming out till late in the night but he was seen by none, since he had parked his car in a desolate corner, could only be seen when looked for.

Madan reached Delhi railway station in the morning, just carrying a small hand bag with him, dressed in white kurta-pyjama and slippers. Though he had to wait for the train going to Haridwar (UP) for about 3-4 hours at Delhi railway station, but not even once did he remember of his good days as one of the top industrialists of Delhi. He was nearly a total renunciate, obsessed with a very noble aim. Nothing could disturb him at this stage. He caught the train from Delhi, for Haridwar. Having reached Haridwar late in the evening, he went to one of the free Dharamshalas, of which he knew earlier. This town of Haridwar was not new to Madan since he had visited this in his earlier days for attending religious functions. Of course that time he stayed in the best hotels and lot many people to look after him. But these discomforts now, did not bother him even once. In fact he was happier and more relaxed in that free environment on the bank of the Ganges.

Haridwar is a religious town on the road to Dehradun from Delhi. The name of this town has a great significance since it means 'Gate to God'. The Ganges which emenates from Gangotri in Uttranchal (in the Garhwal region) touches Haridwar as the first township after it leaves the Hirnalayan ranges and enters the plains. There are a large number of temples in this area including legendary 'Sapt Rishi' (seven Saints) and Bheem Goda ashrams. As per Hindu scriptures and Vedas a human being should gradually get detached during Van Prashat (after 50 years) of age and then should finally renunciate the world and take on to Sanyas (after 75 years of age). There are two seprate ashrams for both these stages ie Van prashat ashram and Sanyas ashram. It is a strong belief that once one reaches Haridwar, for sincerely seeking liberation (mukti) from the birth and death cycle, is already halfway to Astral world.

There are periodical religious congregations known as 'kumbh ka mela' where lacs of people from all over the country come to this town to have a dip in holy river Ganges. There are some other occasions when people come for taking bath in the Ganga which as per belief absolves one of all sins and also ones desires are fulfilled. The 'ashes' of the dead are also immersed into the Ganges with a belief that after this ritual one's soul gets 'mukti'. There are different Pandits for different areas who keep and maintain records of family trees of the entire country; ether by physically going around their respective areas or from the people who keep coming with the ashes of their near and dear ones. It is indeed a Hari (God) Dwar (Gate) Haridwar.

Next day, Madan went to one of the 'Math's (religious place) to attend morning aarti (religious discourse) and spent most of his day there only. In fact he made it his routine to spend most of his time in that temple in the services of God and also ate from the langar there only.

Since Madan was a regular visitor to the temple of 'lord Krishna' he was noticed by the Poojari (Priest) who was also very old around 80 years of age and had seen number of disciples come and go. But he found Madan an old person of about 70 Years of age, fully devoted and sincere towards his Karmas in service of God. From the general grace conduct and behavior of Madan, the priest could know that Madan was a person from a very rich background and now has taken on to complete 'Sanyas'. There was something fonitcal and saintly in Madan's appearance.

"Bhagat ji (Sanyasi) please come here, I want to talk to you," The priest asked Madan after the pooja.

Madan got up and went to the priest and sat next to him as asked for by the Priest.

"Where have you come from? It is your permanent renunciation or having been troubled by an event or circumstances you are here for a temporary relief," Further asked Priest.

"I am here on the orders of the Almighty. It is time for me to devote rest of the life in the service of God. He has been very kind to me through out my life now the time has come that I also do something in His service," Replied Madan very humbly.

The Priest was very delighted to listen to Madan, whom he found to be a true devotee; a total renunciate. His serenity and peace made Madan look angle in nature. The priest employed him suitably in the 'math' and a routine to perform religious discourses and going to 'Har Ki Pori' (stairs leading to bank of the Ganges) had set for Madan. Madan was now fully engrossed in his new profile and was fully happy in the new environment. He had changed his robes also to saffron and had become 'baba Madan Giri' from Madan lal.

About two years had past. Madan had found a place for his liberation from the bondage of his life; undisturbed by anything. One day after the morning 'aarti' he was going down the 'Har ki Podi' that he was intercepted by some one.

"Uncle Madan, Namaste, I am Kishan from village Rajgarh", Said a young man accompanied by his wife standing on the 'Har ki Podi'."

Madan was surprised, yet happy to hear once again the name of his birth place Rajgarh.

I am sorry my child, I have not recognized you," Asked Madan.

"I am son of Sarpanch Rampat of village Rajgarh, she is my wife, we came to attend 'kumbh ka mela' and now we are on our way back to Rajgarh," Said Kishan, introducing himsef.

Madan was slightly emotionally moved and took the couple to one side, in the varanda of the ashram, there only Kishan told him about the entire happenings after Madan left Rajgarh, unannounced. Madan even enquired about the state of community welfare projects he had started and was happy to know that these were doing well as he had wished. Finally he blessed the couple and earnestly asked them not to tell about his whereabouts to anyone, that would un-do his entire karmas offered in the services of the God. The couple having promised to abide by the wishes of Madan left for Rajgarh. Madan now was stead-fast and was not susceptible to emotional feelings.

Madan returned to the temple. Performed his daily routine of the day. He was slightly uneasy. He kept on thinking the whole night about meeting the son of sarpanch Rampat at 'Har ki Podi'. Though Madan had asked the young man Kishan not to divulge about his whereabouts but he was not sure if Kishan or his wife would be able to keep it with them for a long time. And if that happens the complete gram panchayat of Rajgarh and a few others would reach Haridwar and force him to return to Sikar/Rajgarh. This thought was troubling him the whole night.

Madan got up early in the morning as usual, went to the 'math' performed his religious pooja etc. The Priest was also around, who noticed Madan slightly morose. When the morning activities got over, the Priest sent for Madan to his room which was in the complex of the temple itself.

Priest—Madan come and sit down. Are you all right? I have not seen you in such a sad mood during the last two years that you have been here with us.

Madan—No, there is nothing much. It is just like that; a very small incident but it did put me off, a little.

Madan narrated the complete incident to the Priest and expressed his apprehensions of people coming from his village and forcing him to return. Though Madan was sure of no return from here, but he did not want any kind of embarrassments on this account to anyone. Madan while thinking of a way out of this problem, found leaving Haridwar as the only viable solution.

Madan—The only way out is to leave Haridwar with your permission and go to some other place in Himalayas.

Priest—Yes, Madan these are the hazards of 'Garasth ashram' which you have just left. I also agree with you that before you are mentally disturbed, you should move out of this place. You don't have to go to Himalayas for this, I shall send you to our other 'ashram' which as four kilometers from here. I think that should meet the requirement.

Madan—No, they will be able to locate me there. In any case that fear will always haunt me in the same town, of being identified again by some one, known to me from my past life.

Priest—What do you plan then. Tell me, I shall do anything for you.

Madan—I want to go to 'Badri Nath' or 'Kedarnath' in the mountains, where I feel no one will ever be able to disturb me.

Priest—OK, Madan, I shall let you go to Badri Nath (Tapoban), up in the Himalayas. You will certainly find that place more peaceful and conducive to meditation. There is a small ashram there; my Guru who is now 100 years of age, lives there. I shall give you a reference note. You go and meet him, he is a true saint, will show you the way to seek liberation. His ashram is just on the bank from where river Saraswati emanates. The small area is known as Mana, very close to Bheem pul (Bhim bridge) which was reportedly launched by Bheem of Pandvas while crossing the water channel during there final ascend to Himalayas. Badri Nath Shrine is just three kilometers from there, a walking distance."

Madan was feeling relieved of tension and was happy. He planned to leave the next day, as per the advice of the priest without telling anyone else in the 'Math' about his change of place.

Next day, Madan got up early morning and caught a bus for Badri Nath, again not to return to Haridwar ever.

VII

Madan having travelled the whole day in a bus reached Badrinath in the evening. It was getting slightly dark and a bit cold being the higher altitude. Fortunately Madan found some one at the bus stand itself going to Mana village and he knew the 'Ashram' of Saint Durga Dass' where Madan had to go.

Madan went along with that person to the Ashram. It took about half an hour to reach there from the bus stand. The area was giving a deserted look, surrounded by high Himalayan ranges, clad with snow all around. The weather was pleasant since it was a summer month. There was a small light visible at a distance. The man accompanying Madan indicated that to be the entry to Saint Durga Dass Ashram.

It was already 8 PM when Madan reached that Ashram. On entering the Ashram he met two more disciples of Saint Durga Dass, who were in their forties and young looking, clad in saffron.

Seeing Madan, an old man also in saffrons, the disciples quickly attended to him.

"Yes, baba what can we do for you," Asked one of the disciples.

"I want to meet Saint Durga Dass, I am coming from Haridwar, Priest Sham Giri has sent me here," Very politely replied Madan.

"Come in-side and sit down, we will get you some tea, it is slightly cold here, this time of the day," Said one of the disciples.

"I am Ram Dass and he is Laxman Dass, the younger one," further introduced the elder of the two.

"May I meet the Guru ji now," Asked Madan.

"He goes to sleep early and wakes up very early around 4 AM everyday. You can meet him only in the morning now," Said Ram Dass.

"Do not worry, we have enough arrangements here in the ashram to eat and sleep, Sadhus often keep coming here from Badrinath," Further said Ram Dass.

Madan was offered self cooked food by the disciples and was accommodated for the night. Madan had a sound sleep since he was old and had got tired travelling the whole day in the bus in mountainous terrain. He also got up early in the morning but by then Guru ji (Saint Durga Dass) was already up and doing his pooja. Madan quickly got ready to be called by the Guru ji.

"Come Madan Giri," Said guru ji sitting outside.

Madan went to him, paid normal respect and sat down as was asked by the guru ji. Madan then took out a piece of paper which the Priest from Haridwar had given him for the Guru ji. The Guruji read the note and kept it in his pocket.

"Welcome Madan, you have come to the right place, but slightly late in life. Do not worry for those who sincerely seek Him, it is never late," Said Guruji.

Guruji briefed his disciples about Madan a renunciate and asked them to accomodate him in one room.

The Ashram was located in a valley, on one side snow capped Himalayas offered their protection and on other side a thick forest of pine trees sprouted a perfectly natural tribute to this enchanting fantasy land.

Next day Madan was taken around by one of the disciples to acquaint him with the area. In fact this was the beginning of his attaining salvation. Madan was very happy to have found a learned and knowledge Guru ji in Saint Durga Dass. Madan requested Saint Durga Dass who was now about 105 years old to accept him as one of his disciples. Guruji with his experience had already sensed the potential in Madan and happily accepted him as his disciple.

Though Madan was not new to the religious drills and ethos since he had already spent two years at Haridwar, yet Guruji started briefing Madan from the beginning.

The Guru ji started briefing Madan as the time past as follows:-

Firstly, "Learn to control your mind, Madan. It is difficult to control a restless mind, but by practice and firm resolve you can restrain it and successfully wean it away from the sense objects and turn it inwards in quest of Self Realisation. The mind is only the cause of man's bondage and it is also the mind which is the instruments of man's liberation.

Secondly "Madan Spirituality means total surrender of your egos, identification, individualism and only then one can seek liberation. The spiritual seeker sees wordly joys and happiness as detraction from the quest for the eternal bliss within."

Thirdly, "What is needed is absorption of God, loving Him intensely. God is the lake of Nector, the ocean of immoratality. Sinking in it one does not die but verily transcends death."

Fourthly, "This world is a place of miseries where everything is temporary and where no lasting happiness can be found. Vedanta says that our very essence is bliss and the moment we try to increase it from external source our miseries begin."

Fifthly, "The soul dwelling within this body is always identified with God. It is free from body and mind of human beings. It can not be destroyed by any means. He who establishes relation with his soul attains the vision of immortality and reaches the supreme state. Spiritual development can only be achieved through deep meditation. After death the 'soul' departs to its heavenly abode, on high or low plane depending on the 'Karmas' of an individual on earth. Only a very few are able to seek liberation from the death and birth cycle, such Soul on departure merges with the God."

This is broadly I have given out the concept and philosophy of this life and the nature; If you need to ask me anything in particular, do so, asked the Guruji from Madan.

"Yes, Guruji I have generally got you well and shall adhere to your advice and guidance, I think this much should meet my requirement," Submitted Madan.

"Madan I have grown too old and may depart anytime now. You have been here for over an year in the ashram doing your meditation. After I leave you have to fit in my slot as a Saint, I shall therefore tell you the qualities and virtues a Saint possesses," Said Guruji. "Yes, Guruji, but I am a very small human being to attain that status. But your advice may help me in reaching that level," Said Madan.

Guruji— "A Saint or a yogi is one who has successfully attained spirituality and has become master soul. He also helps people to seek liberation from the cycle of death and birth. A Saint bestows spirituality as a gift to mankind and is a living embodiments of humility. His association releases in us currents of bliss and benediction. Everyone who comes to a Saint whether a devotee or a sinner, derives benefit in his own way and gets solace from him. But this all comes to a saint when he totally detaches himself from the wordly affairs, total renunciation, deep meditation in solitary confines thus knowing the self (soul). This way he establishes a link with the God and attains ultimate liberation."

Madan was a very sincere bhakt who by now had attained almost all those qualities of a saint which the Guruji had spelt out to him. Guruji also expressed his will to nominate Madan as his successor.

Two years past—

One day a disciple came running to Madan at 3 AM in the morning informing him that guruji was very restless and sinking. Madan went running and sat near the guruji, who was unable to speak at that stage. Madan realized that the time for guruji had come to leave us. It so happened after a few minutes the guruji departed, putting his hand on the head of Madan giri.

VIII

Madan took on the responsibilities of the ashram well. He had fully understood ad realized the Self. Madan spent most of the time in meditation, even sometimes for days together, without food and water in a solitary place within the ashram. Madan metamorphosed into a complete Saint. His serenity and piece of mind made him look godly in nature and enlightened in substance.

The disciple found a total change in Madan over a period of time. He had become a very godly person. He gave out his views on life and eternity before disciples. His disciples got hypnotized with his eloquence, knowledge and wisdom. Guru Durga Dass used to move out to Badrinath shrine very often but Madan had restricted it to special occasions only. His belief was that this entire complex is Badrinath abode; He resides in our hearts, one should only have to know, how to awaken Him. He advised people that those who study others are wise and those who study the 'self' are enlightened. Enlightened people do not compete with others, they compete with 'self' for betterment.

Madan's fame as a complete Saint spread all-round. His every sentence provoked admiration during discourse.

Even Mehant of the Badrinath started visiting Madan. At times there used to be larger gatherings of people at the ashram than at Badrinath's shrine. Madan was a totally selfless person and afforded sincere advice and guidance to the people without stint, who-so-ever approached him.

One day an English man, Mr Peter Ken, businessman by profession, forced to confront the spiritual crises of his out of balance life, reached Tapoban (badrinath) area looking for mental peace and salvation. He learnt about Saint Madan Giri, being a Master Soul and reached his ashram located in a defile at Mana, to seek spiritual guidance for transformation of his overburdened life. Next day Mr Peter Ken went to Mana and attended the normal religious discourse in the morning at the ashram, but stayed behind to meet Saint Madan Giri after all others had dispersed. Saint Madan Giri noticed a foreigner still sitting on a bench in one corner of the ashram, looking lost in wilderness with totally innocent disposition. He asked one of his disciples to help the English man if he wanted to be shown around. But on enquiry it was revealed that he wanted to meet the Saint in person to seek certain clarifications to overcome maladies of human life and accordingly he was allowed to meet Saint Madan Giri.

"Yes, what help could I be to you," Asked the Saint from the English man.

"My name is Peter Ken. I am from London (England). I am very successful man in business, but without mental peace. I have known about the wisdom of Indian seers and that is why I am here in your ashram with certain questions pertaining to human life. If your holiness permits, I shall proceed," Spoke the English man.

"Please proceed, Mr Peter Ken with God's permission I shall try to meet your requirement," Said the Saint.

Q. "Life of a 'House Holder' (gharasthi), irrespective of his social and financial standing, is very complex and at times leads to frustration. How do you address this", Asked Mr Peter Ken.

"In today's materialistic world human being attach more importance to amassing wealth and gathering other things which add to their domestic pleasure. He has no time for the Almighty in his scheme of things. Gharasth ashram is described by our Seers as the supreme and is the most important of all the ashrams (others being Brahamcharya, up to age of 25 years, Van parsath after 50 years of age and finally Sanyas after 75 years of age). The path of the house holder has always been a most challenging path. Perhaps the most challenging. It is easy to want nothing when you are only dealing with yourself. It is natural, when you have others, you love, to want only the best for them, food, clothing and education etc. But the trouble begins when one starts making money over and above his needs, for the posterity. This is a stage where one can exercise control over lust, greed and other un-ethical vices and practise time tested values of honesty, sincerity, love, courtesy, compassion and concern for others," Told the Saint.

"Learn to control your mind. It is the source of all your actions good or bad. Lord Krishna tells in Bhagvad Gita that mind is like a horse if controlled it will take your directly to God failing which the human being will become centre of the sufferings," Further said the Saint.

"Be karam yogi (good deeds) as a house holder. Lord Krishna further tells in Bhagvad Gita that all karmas (deeds) must be done as a sacrifice in the devotion to God; all actions unless done in an offering to God become causes of bondage," Further explained the Saint.

"Birth, death, loss, gain and illness etc in the family go on as per his stipulations and rules. These are pre-ordained by Him for each individual as per his past deeds. Also the pursuit of excellence in any physical area is meaningless and short-lived unless the emotional, spiritual and mental sides of our lives are fully developed. Do not grieve over your present state, have faith in God, He will show you the way," Explained the Saint.

"As regards our near and dear ones are concerned, we have established strong family ties, least realizing that the relations one has in this life are only with this body which keep changing with every life. The relations one has today were never there in one's past life, nor would they be there in the next life. Everyone has come to perform his duties assigned by God and would disappear thereafter. You do not recall your past life and do not remember as to who all cried on your death, same would happen here. Your close and dear ones will soon forget you, this is the law of nature," Briefed the Saint.

Q. "From your conversation I realize that there is a re-incarnation for everyone. Is it so," Asked Peter Ken.

"Soul is immortal, never dies and it is your body which is perishable. The human soul mostly lies burried under immense load of material pressure. Man is clothed in ignorance and all his actions too are born of ignorance. This keeps him in bondage of vicious cycle of life and death; till his karmas get him finally liberated; after which the soul merges with God. The soul dwelling within this body is always identified with God. The soul existed before the birth of the body and will remain after the death of this body. Nobody is born or dies at any time it is the mind that conceives its birth and death and its migration to other bodies and other world. As long as we continue to identify life in terms of body, mind, intellect, we shall remain enslaved to our subtle tendencies. If we get rid of this, it will get us out of the vicious cycle of birth and death. Some souls are reborn, of souls which get out, go to astral world and merge with the Absolute and there is no rebirth thereafter," Saint Madan Giri explained.

"You westerns may find it hard to imagine re incarnation. There have been so many reports from thoroughly, reliable sources of the past life experiences. Some of these people have brought back strickingly detailed description of events, and such completely verifiable data as to eliminate any possibility that they were making it up or had contrived to somehow deceive researchers and loved ones," Further added the Saint.

Q. "What is Spirituality? How does one go about attaining liberation," Asked Mr Peter Ken from the Saint.

"Spirituality means total surrender of your ego, identifications, individualism and then only one can seek liberation. The spiritual seeker sees wordly joys and happiness as a detraction from the quest for eternal bliss within. The eternal is not obtained by rites or rituals, by pilgrimages nor by wealth, it is to be obtained by controlling one's mind and cultivating wisdom. The path of Spirituality is strewn with difficulties and can not be safely trod except with the help and guidance of a master soul. Spirituality is all about inner purity where love is un conditional, faith is undivided and the mind is above matters. It has the freedom to establish direct link with the Absolute divine power. It does not belong to any sect or religion. God makes no difference between men, place and time. He is omnipresent. He will respond to anyne's call, if such call is with love and full faith, devoid of cunning," Explained the Saint.

Q. "Is Renunciation part of Spirituality," Asked Mr Peter Ken.

"Yes, because ultimately all Spirit renounce what is not real and nothing in this life is real except the God. Yet renunciation in the classic sense of self denial is not required. A true follower does not give up something, he simply sets aside. Often a person on spiritual path looks like he has renounced all earthly passion, all human desire. What he has done is understand it, see the illusion and step aside from the passions which do not serve him. The renunciate never denies passion–the renunciate simply denies attachment to results. They live ones life without expectations, without need for specific results, that is freedom. That is Godliness. Renunciation is not a decision to deny action. Renunciation is a decision to deny a need for particular result. The renunciate seeks to end separation between him and God through meditation. This is oneness and union with God; a melding with and melting into divinity. The renunciate therefore renounces results but never, ever renounces passion. Indeed he knows intuitively that passion is a path. It is the way to Self Realization," Spoke Saint Madan Giri.

Mr Peter Ken who looked little composed and relieved said, "There is nothing more I could ask. I am filled with thanks for this incredible dialogue with your holiness. It has been so far reaching and so encompassing". He left the ashram fully indoctrinated after listening to the Saint on the philosophy of human life.

Time passed, Madan was getting old but Saintly. One day Madan got up early morning as usual and finished his normal routine. He was looking very happy and cheerful. He took his disciples with him to Badrinath shrine that afternoon. During the whole day he was explaining to his disciples as to what should they do incase he had to leave this world one day.

After normal meals Baba Madan Giri went to sleep at about 8 PM as usual. It was a special night for Madan. He, while still trying to sleep, saw a bright light emenating from the corner of his room. Saint Madan Giri sat up on his bed with folded hands staring at that light. The light soon changed into the figure of Lord Krishna, the God, which though was not clearly visible due to darkness in the room but the movement of Lords hands were reasonably well seen. Madan Giri was highly delighted to see that with his 'atut bhakti' (extreme meditation) and devotion, he was able to win that favour of Almighty's darshan (glimpse of God). He started praying in front of the God. The God asked Madan to stop praying and listen to Him carefully. God told him "You have completed your job on this earth well and now time has come for you to depart to heavenly abode. I am very happy with your 'Karmas' and your soul will get liberated from this bondage of death and birth cycle. In fact you were to attain liberation in your last birth itself when I sent you to the church. But it was found that your 'karmas' were still incomplete and you were to undergo yet another cycle of garasth ashram, that is why I called you back early from there. I tested you a number of times, once when you lost everything including your father; when you lost your wife and in laws in the car accident and then when you were insulted by your daughter in law, but at no time you lost faith in Me which sustained you in these calamities. Now that you have performed well to my satisfaction I shall take you with Me to astral world to stay there for ever," Having said that the God disappeared, so did Saint Madan Giri once for all.

Next day morning when the disciples saw Baba Madan Giri still sleeping they got suspicious and went to his room, only to find that the Baba had already departed to Heavens.

❑❑❑

The God: Know Him
(Excepts from the Bhagwad Gita)

Lord Krishna Tells Arjuna:-

I am the primal causè of all creations and the eternal seed of all beings. There is nothing else besides Me. Even the gods and the great seers emanate from Me. I know the past, the present and the future. Yet neither the sages and gods, nor this world in delusion know Me as the unborn and immutable.

I am not manifest to all, because I am beyond all factors and forces, birth less and one without a beginning. Keeping my creations under control and through my 'Yoga Maya'. I manifest myself and he who knows Me is freed from the recurring courses of births and deaths.

I am the Self (Atman) residing in all. I am the source (creator), the middle (sustainer) and the end destroyer. There is nothing anywhere either moving or stationary that exists without Me.

I am ever glorious and divine in My incarnation and he who knows this truth and understands as well, My supreme glory and supernatural powers attains Me only, he is not reborn.

The Seven great Seers (Marichi and others), the more ancient four (Sanaka and others) and the fourteen 'Manus' (progenitors of mankind), all of them powerful and devoted to Me, are born of My will.

Arjuna; I am the upholder of dharma. So whenever dharma declines and unrighteousness is on the ascent, and also when there is need for protection of the virtuous and destruction of the evil-doers and re establishment of dharma, I manifest Myself of My own free will.

I am Vishnu among the Adityas and radiant Sun among the luminaries. I am Marichi, the glorious, among the Maruts and Moon among the stars.

I am Samaveda among Vedas, Indra among the Gods, mind among the sense organs and consciousness in the living beings. I am Kubera. I am Agni among the Vasus and Meru among the mountains.

Among priest I am Brihaspati: I am Skanda among warriors and among sheets of water I am ocean.

I am Bhrigu among the great seers and the words I am the monosyllable "OM". Of Yagnas I am japa Yagna and among the sturdy immovable I am Himalayas. Of trees I am the Aswathla tree. Among horses I am Uichchaishravas; of lordly elephants I am Airavatha and amongst men I am the king. I am wind among elements that purify; I am Rama among the wielder of weapons; among fishes I am Makara and among rivers I am the Ganges. Of the weapons, I am thunderbolt and among cows I am Kamadhenu; of poisonous snakes I am Vasuki; among aquatic beings I am Varuna. I am Aryaman among the men and Yama (god of death) among those that regulate, control and rule; and I am Ananta among non-venomous snakes.

Among the Daityas I am Prahlad, among reckoner I am Time. I am the lion among quadrupeds and Garuda among birds. I am the productive passion, and among disputants in argument I am dispassionate reasoning. In the alphabet I am Akram which is also the first sound in Oms; of compounds in grammar I am the cupulative compound.

I am the sprout for everything that comes into being; I am the Goddess of wealth (Lakshmi) and the goddess of learning (Saraswati) among women. I am the presiding deity over the forces and influences of steadfastness of mind, power of memory, intelligence and retention of memory and also fame and forbearance.

I am Brhatsaman in the Vedic hymns, Gayatri in mantras, Margasirsha in the months of the year and of the season of the year I am spring. I am the game of disc among those that deceive, the prowess of the powerful, and the victory of those victorious. I am effort and goodness (Satvan) in good natured people.

I am Vasudeva (Krishna) among the vrishnis and Arjuna among Pandavas; I am Vyasa of the sages and amongst the wise I am Sage Sukara (usana kavi).

I am the ruling power in the rulers; righteousness or right policy I am, for those aspiring victory; wisdom in the wise and of secrets I am silence.

I am the sustainer of all the universal dispenser of the fruits of action and justice. I am all the powerful and the inexorable force of death and eternal time.

I am the Lord of all, the supreme goal, protector, friend and an unattached witness. I am the abode, an asylum, a retreat for those that surrender unto Me; the resting place and the repository into which all beings merge at the time of dissolution.

I am Omipresent, omniscent and ommipotent.

Who Can Reach Unto God

Lord Krishna Says:-

Neither by a study of the Vedas, nor by performance of rituals, sacrifices and austerties, nor by offering of gifts am I seen. It is he who constantly established in the 'path of devotion' that attains immortality and bliss transcending all.

And, I speedily rescue from the ocean of transmigatory existence beset with birth and death those pious devotees who constantly worship Me with devotion also surrounding unto Me the fruits of their actions.

Of all I consider those who keep their minds even on Me devoutly with supreme faith to be best of the Yogis. However, even the others who are self controlled, even minded and devoted to doing good to all living beings and who adores the eternal all pervading unmanifest Brahma which is beyond all comprehension, attain Me.

But this path to the unmanifest is more ragged and it is attained only with difficulty by an embodied being. Therefore resort to the yoga of equanimity, resign mentally all actions to Me, fix your mind and intellect on Mr alone. When you abide in Me only, I redeem you from the course of repeated births and deaths.

If, however, you are unable to do so, then seek to attain Me by yoga of a sustained practice of your choice. If you are unable to take up this course, then be intent on performing "actions solely for my sake".

Again if you are unable to resort to this yoga of action or actions for My sake, then take refuge in Me in self control, renounce the fruits of all actions in My favour, because this is by far the best.

Men of wisdom devoutly worship Me with their mind intellect and their very lives on Me. Knowing Me as the supreme, they sing My glory, propagate same amongst themselves in the spirit of service and remain happy lot in this way of life and pursuit deriving the bliss of their devotion.

Just to bless them I dwell in the hearts of those ever devoted to Me in their worship and love: Of My own, I dispel the darkness of their ignorance by the light of knowledge. I shower My grace upon them and in that illuminated state of total integration, the yoga of the intellect (Budhi yoga), they attain Me only.

Alike the pain and pleasure, friend and foe, honour and dishonour, good and evil praise and censure, hot and cold, forgiving by nature, of firm resolve, contemplative and ever contented; mind set on Me and self dedicated to Me – such person is dear to Me.

The pious one from whom others get no trouble, and he who gets no trouble, either, from the world; the one who is equanimous and free from elation, anger, fear, anxiety and all other mental afflications; one who neither desires, nor rejoices, nor hates or grieves, who is impartial, craves not but continues to performs the ordained duties–who is dexterous, pure internally and externally, has not particular attachment to home–such a person is dear to Me.

Surely, those who faith and fervour, who take recourse to this path of devotion and actually practice this science of high spiritual value, keeping Me as their supreme goal are also very dear to Me.

Who even offers Me with sincere love a leaf, a flower, a fruit or even water for that matter–that I delightfully partake off.

So offering unto Me by way of love, devotion and dedication whatever you do, eat or give away as gift–be rid of the good and evil consequences of actions (karmas): and on Me fix thy mind, to Me bring thy devotion: to Me make thy obeisance; by this way, to Me, indeed thou shall surely come.

Renunciation of actions and performance of actions–both are good, as they lead to the same goal. But performance of actions is superior to renunciation, because that ideal state of renunciation of action is difficult to achieve without yoga in action. As for renunciation it is not possible for the embodied beings to completely disown all actions as such; so he who relinquishes "the fruit of actions" is indeed a true relinguisher (tyagi).

Devotion to own duty is glorified. It leads one to perform and it is as efficacious as worshipping the God, from whom all this creation has emanated, and by whom all this is pervaded.